THE CELTIC CROSS SERIES

Part 2, Ireland:
The Pursuit of Peace
Epoch 9

THE FAMISHMENT OF THE PEOPLE

Of Hunger and Fulfillment

DONNA FLETCHER CROW

Author of *Glastonbury, The Novel of Christian England*

The Famishment of the People,
Of Hunger and Fulfillment
Epoch 9, The Celtic Cross Series
Part II, Ireland: The Pursuit of Peace

Copyright © 2022 by Donna Fletcher Crow
All rights reserved as permitted under the U.S. Copyright Act of 1976.

No part of this publication may be reproduced or transmitted in any form
or by any means, electronic or mechanical, including photocopy recording
or any information storage and retrieval system, without permission in
writing from the publisher. The only exception is brief quotations in
printed reviews.

Verity Press
Boise

Cover design and format by Ken Raney
Edited by Sheila Deeth
This is a work of fiction. The characters and events portrayed in this book
are fictitious or used fictitiously.

Published in the United States of America
Adapted from *The Banks of the Boyne*
A Quest for a Christian Ireland
Copyright © 1998 by Donna Fletcher Crow
Moody Press
Chicago

Part II, Ireland, permissions

Four lines from "In Memory of Eva Bore-Booth and Con Markievicz" *The*

Collected Works of W. B. Yeats, Volume 1: The Poems, Revised, Editor: Richard J. Finneran. U. S. rights, Simon & Schuster, used by permission.

Extracts from *The Land of Heart's Desire,* "The Stolen Child," "The Lake Isle of Innisfree," and "In Memory of Eva Gore-Booth and Con Markievicz" from *The Collected Poems of W. B. Yeats.* Permission of A. P. Watt Ltd. on behalf of Michael Yeats.

"Bind Us Together," by Bob Gillman, 1977 Kingsway's Thankyou Music/adm. in North, South and Central America by Integrity's Hosanna! Music/ASCAP. All rights reserved. International copyright secured. Used by permission.

"Rejoice," by Graham Kendrick, 1983 Kingsway's Thankyou Music/adm. in North, South and Central America by Integrity's Hosanna! Music/ASCAP. All rights reserved. International copyright secured. Used by permission.

Quotations (letters) from *The Life and Time of Mary Ann McCracken 1770-1866* by Mary McNeill. Permission: Blackstaff Press Ltd., Belfast: 1988.

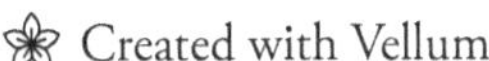 Created with Vellum

England my passion,
Scotland my joy,
Ireland my pain.

To all who have
suffered for Ireland

THE CELTIC CROSS SERIES

Part 1 Scotland: The Struggle for a Nation

Epoch 1
The Keeper of the Stone,
Of Saints and Chieftains

Epoch 2
The Forger of a Nation,
Of Kings and Kingdoms

Epoch 3
The Refiner of the Realm,
Of Queens and Clerics

Epoch 4
The Vanquishers of Tyranny,
Of Priests and Patriots

TIMELINE

THE GENERATIONS OF NORTHERN IRELAND

Generation 1—The Plantations
1607 The Flight of the Earls
1610 The plantation of Ulster begins
1611 King James Bible published

Generation 2—Cromwellian Ulster
1625 Charles I crowned
1639 The Black Oath required
1641 The Uprising
1649 Charles I beheaded, Cromwell takes Drogheda

Generation 3—The Ascendancy
1689 The Siege of Londonderry
1690 The Battle of the Boyne
1695 First of the Penal Laws enacted

1717 First wave of Irish emigration to America

Generation 4—The Union

1789 John Wesley's last visit to Ireland

1791 Wolfe Tone forms United Irishmen

1798 Rising against English rule

1801 Dublin and Westminster Parliaments united

Generation 5—The Great Famine

1845 First potato crop failure

1859 Evangelical revival sweeps Ulster

Generation 6—The Birth of Northern Ireland

1914 Home Rule for Ireland passed, World War I begins

1916 The Easter Rising, The Battle of the Somme

1921 Northern Ireland Parliament opened, Anglo-Irish Treaty signed

ACKNOWLEDGMENTS

I wrote *The Banks of the Boyne*, from which the epochs of Part II of the Celtic Cross Series are adapted, in 1996-1998 during the hopeful, but still turbulent years leading up to the Good Friday Agreement. Fortunately, although conflicts and disagreements still capture international attention today, progress continues—however slowly. New times and new problems; but always there are people of good will who work for solid solutions.

When I wrote my epic account of Northern Ireland's history I had no idea how much our world was about to change—and with it the revolutionary changes in reading habits. The advent of ebooks and Print on Demand publishing has required shorter manuscripts. And so, technology has required that I do what I was already thinking I would like to do: offer my all-encompassing story in individual volumes.

Likewise, I little foresaw that my "modern" sections

would themselves soon be made history by events in our ever-changing world. Apart from such obvious things as outdated technology, the most glaring example of the march of time is the advent of Brexit and the diplomatic nightmare of border division on this small island. My own dilemma was whether or not to rewrite Mary and Gareth's story to march with today's headlines.

With the realization that life is never static, and any changes I would make to the story would themselves be out of date soon, I have chosen not to "update" these formerly modern sections—which have now been relegated to the status of nostalgia. It's important to remember that history doesn't change—only our interpretation of it—but the stories are there—to inspire or to deplore—all part of the amazing, ever-changing story of humanity.

Mary and Gareth's story is based event by event on the summer of 1996. It was the first time in my life to write an historical novel that required reading the morning newspaper to see what my characters were doing that day.

The CCC is based on an actual center in Belfast, and all major characters in the modern story are based on real people—dear, gracious friends whom I thank from the bottom of my heart. I will always remember with gratitude how they opened their hearts, their homes, and their country to me. Thanks especially to Caroline, David, and Ruth McAfee and Harry and Grace Stevenson. Also thanks to Sir Jocelyn Gore-Booth for his tour of Lissadell House.

In the original volume I invited my readers to join me in praying for the many people and organizations working for reconciliation on both sides of the border, such as Billy and Mena Mitchell at the Local Initiative for Needy Communities (LINC Centre), Ivan and Isobell Miles at the Ark Family Centre, and Pastor Philip McAlister and the Oasis Coffee House.

That invitation remains unchanged. Again, issues and personalities change, but as the frequent refrain in Scripture that pleads, "Pray for the peace of Jerusalem," I ask my readers to Pray for the peace of Ireland.

DFC

2022

IRELAND

Lough Swilly
Rathmullen
Londonderry
Co. Donegal
Glenties
ULSTER
Donegal Bay
Belfast
Sligo
CONNACHT
Drogheda
Dublin
LEINSTER
Glendalough
Limerick
MUNSTER
Kinsale
Provincial boundaries
Northern Ireland

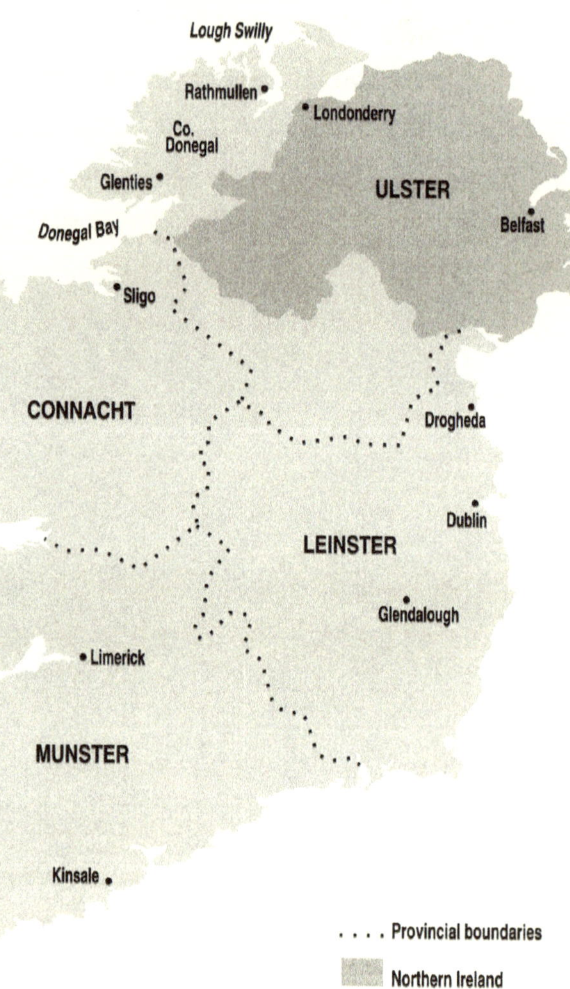

NORTHERN IRELAND

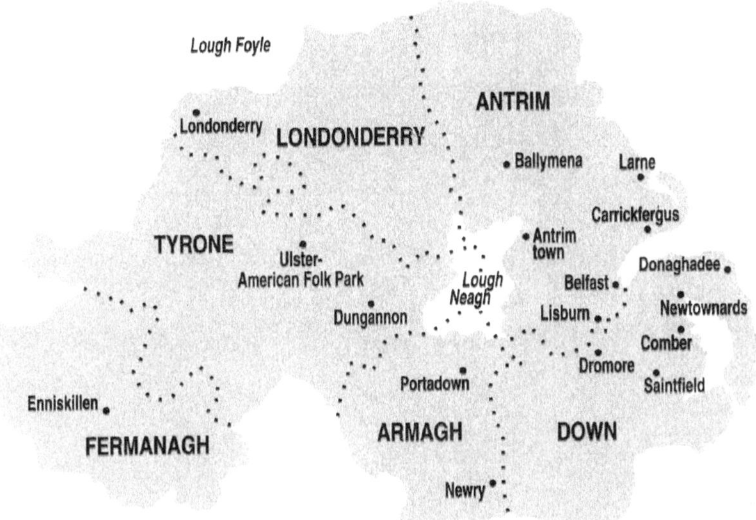

THE GENERATIONS

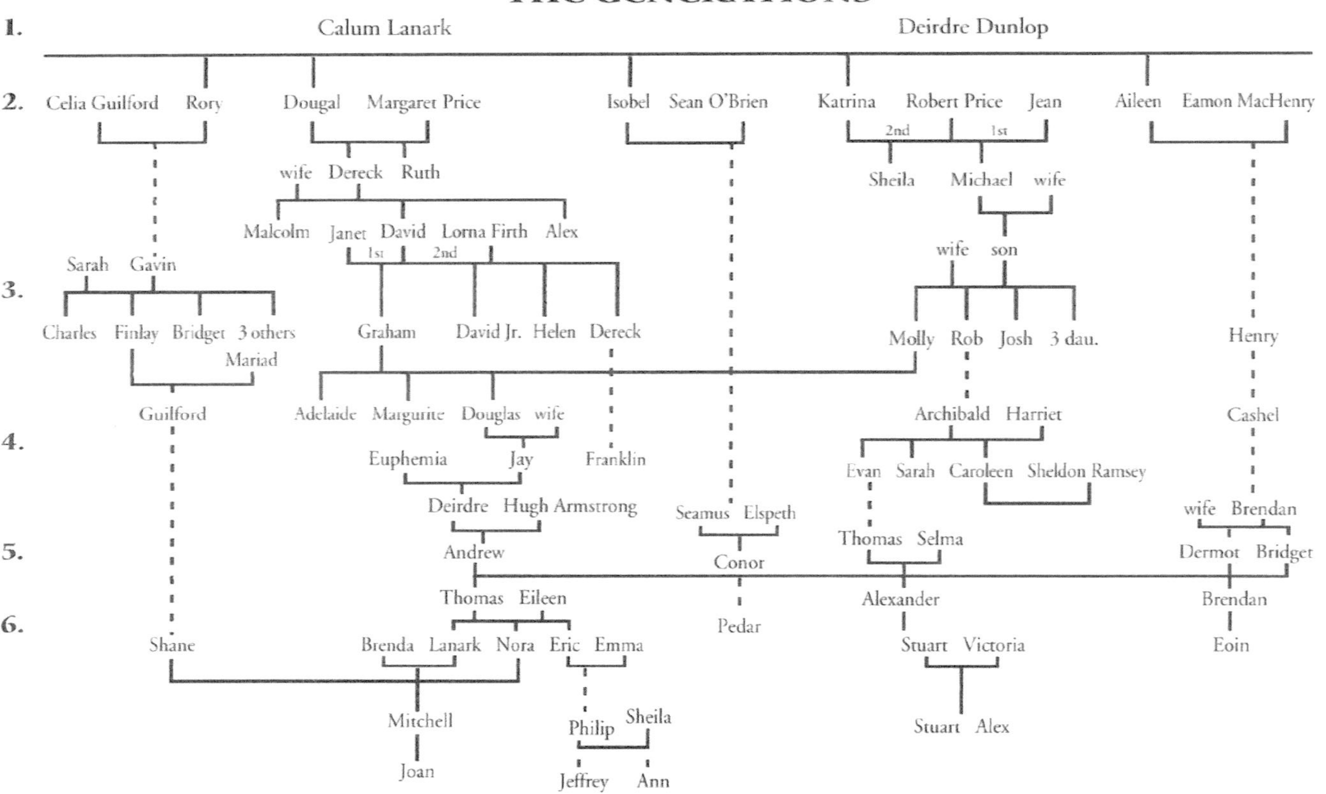

WORD LIST

Except where noted, italicized words are Irish Gaelic. Irish and Scots dialect words are Roman.

abecedarian—rudimentary alphabet book

athair—Irish for father

bairn—babe

bap—bread roll

Battle of Kinsale—1607; England defeated Spain

bawn—fortified enclosure

beannacht—Irish for blessing; a greeting

besom—Scots for obstinate female

biscuits—crisp cookies

Black Oath—oath abjuring the Covenant: required by Charles I

boll—of grain, 6 bushels; of cloth, about 30 yards of fabric

Book of Common Order—by John Knox; regulated worship of the Reformed church

caidleagh; **Scots ceilidh (kay-lee)**—Irish for party; usually with singing and dancing

cailin (**colleen**)—Irish for girl

carrick—man's fashionable greatcoat having multiple capes

chapman—peddler

clachan—cluster of cottages

clairseack, **Scots clarsach**—Irish harp

Clandeboye—ancient Gaelic kingdom, now County Down

coo—cow, Scots dialect

copse—clump of trees, thicket

corbie—Scots for crow

crack—Irish for fun

croppies, cottiers—farmers occupying cottages and small holdings of land in exchange for rent or services

deartháir —Irish for brother

deirfiúr—Irish for sister

dia duit—good afternoon

Deserving Irish—Native Irish who had supported the English Crown in rebellions

dreigh—Scots for gray, drab weather

farl—three-cornered oatcake

Fenian—member of Irish society dedicated to over-throwing English rule

Flight of the Earls—Gaelic lords of Ulster fled to the Continent in 1607, leaving vast lands leaderless

Garda—Irish police

Glorious Twelfth—holiday commemorating Battle of the Boyne (July 1 on old-style calendars; now July 12)

guineaman—gypsy engaged as horse trading agent

hedge school—school held in fields by priests when Catholic education was outlawed

hornbook—a child's primer having a sheet of transparent horn to protect the parchment

Huguenots—French Protestants who suffered persecution in France

inish—island

Jacobite—a supporter of King James and the Stuart line, usually Catholic

landau—elegant four-wheeled carriage

Leveller—political party aimed at leveling all differences of rank

Loyalist—more extreme Unionist

madra (**madoo**)—Irish for dog; used as proper name here

máthair—Irish for mother

National Covenant—Scots confession of faith and denunciation of Charles I

Nationalist—one who wants Northern Ireland to become part of the Republic of Ireland

Old English—English who settled in Ireland during the Middle Ages and became Catholic

partizan—long-handled spear used by foot soldier

plack, merk, groat—small Scottish seventeenth-century coins

plantations—colonies of English and Scots planted in Ireland by the British Crown

rackrent—rent raised on a lease

rapparees—ex-soldiers living as outlaws

Republican—more extreme Nationalist

Rī Sīogaī—Irish fairy king

rieved—stolen

roup—Scots for public auction

Sackville St.—Dublin's main street (now O'Connell)

Scots Confession—first confession of faith by Scots Reformed Church, written by John Knox in 1560

seanchaidh (**she-natchee**)—traditional Scots Gaelic storyteller

seanathair—Irish for grandfather

servitors—former English army officers rewarded with lands to colonize in Ulster

Sinn Fein (**"ourselves alone"**)—Republican political party

stramash, stushie—uproar, Scots dialect

stravaig—to wander aimlessly or to enjoy oneself

ta—Irish for yes

taken up—arrested

termagant—an overbearing woman

the Pale—area of English influence around Dublin in early days (about a forty-mile radius)

Travelers (tinkers)—Irish gypsies of Celtic descent, not Romany

uisce beatha (**"breath of life"**)—Irish for whiskey

uncail—Irish for uncle

undertakers—Protestant colonists who undertook to settle large sections of Ulster

Unionist—one who wants Northern Ireland to remain part of the United Kingdom

wane—baby (also wee'un)

wheesht—be quiet, Scots dialect

woodkerne—outlaw

wrack—seaweed gathered for fertilizer

wrackers—poor people (usually native Irish) who gathered seaweed

THE GREAT FAMINE

GENERATION FIVE
THE GREAT FAMINE
1845-1913

And Moses said, "Fill an omer of manna to be kept
for your generations;
that they may see the bread wherewith
he Lord hath fed you."
For the Lord is good; his mercy is everlasting;
and his truth endureth to all generations.
Exodus 16:32, adapted Psalm 100:5

1996

Mary Hamilton stared at the calendar hanging on the wall beside her bed in her host's home in Belfast. She shook her head to clear it and blinked. That couldn't be right. She pushed herself up to a sitting position and craned her neck to look out the window. Her shoulders sagged and she sighed. The calendar was right. It was August and she was still in Ireland. In spite of all her determination.

She had been absolutely resolved. After the most recent outbreak of sectarian strife over the Glorious Twelfth Orangemen march, after all her work to help the young people at the reconciliation center come together had fallen apart, after...

She had announced it firmly to Gareth. Although her firmness was tempered—as well as spurred—by her concern for him. After all, he had just clomped in sporting a walking cast: the result of injuries from wrestling with the hoodlum who had broken into the reconciliation center where he was sleeping, since she occupied their host's only spare room.

The scene played over and over in her mind: "Gareth, you know it's true—we never signed on to face riots and bombs. We were going to help establish the peace, and build a recreation center for the young people, and…" her voice broke.

She could still feel the warmth of his arms around her as he drew her to him. "Aye, lass, I know. It's true. And you never signed on at all—I dragged you into this. And you've been so brave."

She took a deep breath, determined not to cry. She wasn't going to beg. She was going to announce. "We've done our best—beyond our best. The situation is impossible. We need to go home. Now."

Gareth raised her left hand to his lips and looked meaningfully at the ring he had placed there so recently. "Home?"

"Scotland, of course. You've got your work there. And I've got a wedding to plan." Her voice steadied at the thought. Then, seeing his relief, she grinned. "Silly, you didn't think I meant America, did you?" Now she held up her ring. "You don't get out of your bargain that easily."

So, it had ended in smiles and kisses. But not in packing.

And she still understood so little. She sighed—she

supposed she would never truly understand—certainly not in any way that made logical sense. She had given up on expecting logic on this side of the looking-glass. But she still had more than a hundred years of history to get through if she could at least hope to know what the events meant that she heard such frequent references to. She looked at the stack of hand-written notebooks containing the story of the Lanark family—the product of their host Philip's efforts while in prison. Organizing his family's documents had been therapeutic for him and he had offered them to her in a similar hopeful spirit. She had conquered four volumes of painful accounts—only two more to go—but now she wondered if she would be any wiser when she finished her reading.

She pushed herself off her bed and pulled volume five from the stack. At least it was slimmer than some of them. Did she dare hope it might contain less violence?

She plopped back on her bed, but she didn't begin reading. Her mind was too occupied with events of the past weeks. Ireland was truly a land of contrasts—and not just in its scenery and weather. She thought of the vandalism that threatened to devastate their work at the Centre for Cross-Community Cooperation; and then the way the community had come together from both sides of the street to repair it. She thought of the ugliness and anger she had experienced when she was caught in a riot in downtown Belfast in response to an Orange Order parade; then the beauty and peace she had experienced on their brief respite to Sligo…

Only to be shattered by Liam's violent outburst at the Irish-American Folk Park. Liam. Her favorite troubled teen. And yet there had been that powerful moment when the raging, bleeding Catholic youth had been sheltered in the arms of a Protestant girl who had suffered a loss so similar to his. That was reconciliation at its deepest meaning. That was what she and Gareth had come to work for. And what they had seen all too little of so far.

Still, Liam had returned to their wobbly rehearsals at the center for their production of Yeats' "The Faerie's Child" which was to be the centerpiece of their fund-raiser "A Night in Olde Belfast." Liam seemed to have steadied since the scene at the folk park. He hadn't accepted the counseling he was offered, but neither had he joined the IRA—so far as anyone knew. She had to be thankful for that.

And her effervescent twin sisters Julie and Becca continued to be her strongest allies in bringing the Belfast teens together. Okay, she would admit it—there were glimmers of hope.

Mary looked at her watch. Still plenty of time before tonight's rehearsal. And before Gareth would return from whatever he and Philip were doing to calm tempers and promote some semblance of stability in the community. Her sisters had offered to help their hostess Sheila today in her work at the CCC organizing the art display that was to be another important part of "A Night in Olde Belfast." So that left Mary with plenty of time to put the kettle on and delve into Philip's next journal.

1845

Andrew Armstrong was hungry, but Grandfather was not to be rushed. No matter that Mrs. B would be taking a tray of hot oat bannocks out of the oven for tea even now. Grandfather Lanark seemed to think the potatoes would disappear from the fields if he didn't ride around every acre and look over every ridge of sturdy green plants every day. What was the use of hiring an overseer, Andrew wondered, if one insisted on doing all the overseeing oneself? Especially when one could otherwise be at home enjoying tea.

Sitting easily on his high-spirited horse, seventy-one-year-old Jay Lanark drew a deep breath, expanding his remarkable white beard, and a satisfied smile spread over his wrinkled face. "Yes sir, Andrew, our family has been growing potatoes on this land for two hundred and thirty-five years."

Andrew was surprised he didn't have it down to the number of months and days as well. The fact that Grandfather said "our family" meant that the matter under discussion was one in which to take pride. Any weakness would be referred to as coming from "your family."

Grandfather Lanark made no secret of the fact that it was a sore thing to him that the only heir to Lanarks' Bawn should bear the name Armstrong. Often during Andrew's seventeen years he had been made to feel that it was somehow his fault that Grandfather Lanark's daughter had died giving birth to his only grandchild. Always frail and pale, Deirdre had managed to hang onto life just long enough to marry and bear Andrew—after her alarmingly handsome Hugh Armstrong had run off to sea, which was somehow probably Andrew's fault as well.

But today Grandfather was in a mood to focus on the past glories of the Lanarks, rather than the sins of the Armstrongs. "Yes sir. Your great-great-great…," a wave of his broad hand conjured up an unending line of Lanarks standing tall and proud behind the hills of potatoes, "… grandfather Calum Lanark was the first one to grow tatties in all of Ulster. Right here—on this very soil. Now that's a thing to be proud of, my boy." He squinted his pale blue eyes in a faraway look. "Yes sir, someday you'll be showing this field to your son, my great-grandson. A fine thing, family tradition. Fine. Solid. Something to build on. Never forget that you're a Lanark through and through."

If only Andrew could forget it. It was a curse. Tradition was the curse of the Lanarks. But Andrew was determined. He would not be like the rest of them. He would not be like Grandfather. He would not join the Orange Order, no matter how many times Grandfather recounted the story of his being there when it was formed. "Someday you'll be Grand Master, just like your grandfather." How many times had he heard that? Did he even know anyone who hadn't said that to him?

But it didn't matter. He could hear it a thousand times more. He would not. He'd show them.

"Well, speak up, lad. What do you have to say for yourself, eh? Just look at that field. You've never seen a more beautiful sight, have you? Never a better crop. Yes sir. Irish Blacks—the very best. White skin, firm flesh, high yield. Not a better tattie anywhere. You remember that, lad, when you take over the planting of these fields. Don't you be led astray. We'll have none of those white-skinned Lumpers on Lanark land. Oh, they're high yield all right but poor taste."

Grandfather's mouth curved downward. "Only good for animal feed, they are. The wild Irish eat them readily enough, but I'd not have them on my table. Nor the Cup —difficult to digest. Poor keeper too. Now the Apple tastes well enough, if you like your tatties round and mealy, but they're a poor yield. Of course, they can be mighty tasty drenched in fresh butter—"

Andrew groaned silently. Would his grandfather never quit talking about eating?

"Yes sir, you remember that, young man. Just over four more years and you'll be of age. You can sign the papers on your twenty-first birthday. The day you take the Lanark name, you take the Lanark fields too. And you can see to the planting of the best tatties in all Ireland—and take your place at the Orange Lodge."

Andrew urged Rannock forward with a sharp kick of his heels. He hoped Grandfather wouldn't notice that he hadn't responded. The quicker they got around the field, the quicker he could get home to Mrs. B's teacakes. And the quicker he could get away from having his grandfather's plans for the future dinned into his ears. With luck he could even continue the rounds without their coming to loggerheads.

Grandfather was really a grand old man, Andrew reminded himself, as he did several times each day. Jay Lanark had spent most of his seventy-one years standing firm for the things he believed in. And no seventeen-year-old boy was about to change him now, even if that boy was the old man's only living direct relative.

Jay Lanark would never understand his grandson's ideas and desires. So, what was the use of annoying him? Besides, Andrew didn't understand himself most of the time. Except for his desire to get home to eat.

But the broad man with the mane of shoulder-length white hair was as immovable as Scrabo Hill, which formed the backdrop of his lands. He would not be hurried. "Aye, a fine crop. I think I'll tear down those old byres and build a fine new storehouse. That's another thing, Andrew, my boy—Blacks store well. Good keepers. New storehouses, that's the ticket. Then we'll keep the crop for the best price. Get top price, yes sir. Build onto the house, too, I'm thinking. We'll have one of those fashionable long galleries. Best houses in Belfast have them—no reason we can't have one, too. But I'll not be filling any room in my house with those French and Italian paintings. We'll have good Scots pictures. Raeburn and Mackenzie—they know how to put paint on canvas." His hand thudded on Andrew's slim shoulder. "That's the ticket, lad. Good Scots heritage— never let you down."

Andrew put a hand against his stomach to keep it from growling. If Grandfather was off on the superiority of the Scots, they'd never get home. He toyed with the idea of reminding Grandfather that there had been a time even Scottish skill had failed. But the old man had suffered enough. His beloved wife, Euphemia, died with the birth of their first child—a daughter, not even capable of carrying on the Lanark name. Jay had done his best in naming her Deirdre after the first Lanark wife.

And when it came time for the frail Deirdre to bring Jay Lanark's grandchild into the world, he had insisted that she go to Edinburgh for her lying-in. This was not a matter of fashion—the Anglo gentry in Ireland bought French and Italian art and sent their women to London for confinement. This was good Scots-Irish hardheaded sense. Edinburgh had the best doctors in the world. The only sensible thing was that she have the best care possible for the birthing of the heir to Lanarks' Bawn.

But even the world's best wasn't enough to keep Dierdre Armstrong née Lanark connected to her thin thread of life. It was evident that she would much rather be with her Hugh, who had been lost at sea. And Jay Lanark had bowed his head and hunched his thick shoulders. If God had not foreordained that his daughter should live, then it was nae man's place to quibble with his Maker. Jay had hired a wet nurse from a poor but respectable family, and Andrew Jay Calum Lanark Armstrong had been borne back to Lanarks' Bawn in the comfortable arms of Elfrith Calder and under the protective eye of Jay Lanark. Under which protective gaze he had remained, lo, these seventeen years.

Grandfather's gaze had ever been loving, if rigid, spiced

with occasional flashes of anger and less frequent flickers of humor. But in all those years Andrew had never once doubted his grandfather's deep caring for him or for Lanarks' Bawn. He never doubted that Jay Lanark ever sought the best for both his grandson and his land. And as long as the two interests did not conflict, there would be no problem. But should there ever be conflict, Andrew was in no doubt which held the greater importance for Grandfather.

Thus, Andrew knew that his own destiny must always be subservient to Lanarks' Bawn. The matter was as firmly predestined as the question of his own salvation. Andrew had every desire to repay Grandfather's love and make him happy. But he feared growing up to be like him. The hardness of spirit at the center of the man was a fearful thing. And Andrew had no desire to spend the rest of his life at Lanarks' Bawn, either, growing potatoes and marching in Orange parades.

The trouble was, he didn't know what he did want to do. He just knew there had to be something more. Now he shifted his gaze from the potato field to look out to Strangford Lough. He didn't feel the same pull of the sea that his father must have felt. But Andrew felt a great sympathy for what his father must have undergone. Had Hugh Armstrong been forced to spend his days circling endless fields of potato hills when in his mind he felt the roll of the deck beneath his feet? Had the pale Deirdre chosen the only man in the long line of Andrew's ancestry that had burned with imagination and adventure? Was it his father's blood in him that made Andrew so unfit for his preordained life?

Rannock plodded obediently beside Grandfather's horse as they turned down the long side of the south field. Even the Lanarks' Bawn horses lacked imagination. But how much imagination could Andrew claim for himself? It didn't take much creativity to know what he didn't want to do. His greatest fear was that at the end of the day he would be just as dull as the more than two hundred years of Lanarks before him. A specter rose in his mind—the brown blob of a Lumper potato. Grandfather was talking on about crop yield. Andrew felt he would go mad if he didn't escape.

All he could do was dig his heels into Rannock's flanks and skim past his grandfather's horse on the narrow path. He could outride Grandfather, but he couldn't outride the brown terror in his own mind. He had to get away before it consumed him.

The swift brown Rannock, however, was more practical. He had no brown blob to outrun. He simply wanted his oats. And so they arrived expeditiously at the fine stable that had been Jay Lanark's proudest addition to the estate.

Grandfather was less than a horse's length behind, and they dismounted together. "Now why'd ye do sae daft a thing as to spur away like that, laddie? We'd another whole field to see."

Andrew laid a comforting hand on Rannock. The horse's sides were heaving not only from the run, he suspected, but from the fact that the horse Andrew had raised from a colt had a keen sensitivity to his master's moods. And Andrew was quivering inside.

But honoring Grandfather was one of the hallmarks of Andrew Armstrong's life. He would not blurt out his turmoil. "I'm sorry, Grandfather. I was hungry." And the answer was no prevarication. It was just that there was a hunger in him that had nothing to do with his stomach. If only he knew what it was.

He led Rannock toward the polished mahogany box that bore his name on a brass plate.

"Shall I be taking him for you now?" A freckle-faced lad with a shock of carroty hair skittered out from the shadows.

"Here, now, you be careful, Conor O'Brien, or you'll be startling my horses."

Grandfather's sharp voice was more likely to startle the stable than the boy's exuberance, however. Young Conor's affinity for horses was obvious to man and beast alike. And all five of the blooded animals inhabiting the Lanarks' Bawn stable profited from the careful attentions of this ten-year-old who seemed to leave the stable only for meals.

Andrew smiled at the lad. He could never help looking on Conor as almost a half-brother—after all, the same woman had given them both suck. Elfrith Calder had done the unthinkable and married a native Irish, but six-year-old Andrew hadn't seen why they couldn't continue to be friends.

Grandfather, however, was adamant. She'd made her choice and married a wild Irish—she who knew better. And after he had rescued her from that stinking Dumbiedykes tenement in Edinburgh! Elfrith would never be welcome to cast her shadow again on Lanarks' Bawn.

So Elfrith O'Brien went to live with the cottiers along the shores of Strangford Lough, and Andrew lost his mother for the second time. The Irish grew potatoes to feed their families, and around the edges of their two- or three-acre plots they grew oats or wheat as a cash crop. This was a cash poor country, and there was little one needed that couldn't be had by bartering—except for paying the rent. The corn, of course, was for export only. Potatoes, butter-milk, and an occasional bit of bacon was all a soul needed to eat. And the energetic state of the seemingly numberless children playing around the doors of the clustered cottages testified to the nutritional value of the diet.

Conor, her first-born, was tolerated to muck out the stables—as long as he kept a low profile and never mentioned his mother. He was a good worker. And he was cheap.

Andrew handed his reins to Conor. "Yes. Take care of him, lad." He turned toward the house and saw a visitor's horse in the end stall. "Oh, Tammis is here. When did he come?"

Conor shrugged. All his attention was on Rannock. "Half an hour ago. Maybe more."

Andrew hurried to the house. He was always glad to see his cousin Thomas Price. Tammis, with his round, pink cheeks, curling black hair, dancing blue eyes, and impulsive ways, couldn't have been less like the wiry, sandy-haired perfectionist Andrew, who always thought through every decision at least five times. Happy-go-lucky Thomas was the spoiled darling of a large outpouring of cousins at Price Manor Farm. And although he was four years older than Andrew, he could have passed for four years his junior except for his expansive size.

The visitor jumped to his feet as Andrew and his grandfather entered the warm, brightly lit kitchen where Mrs. B had been plying her guest with cake and buttered buns. Thomas threw out his arms in greeting. "Aye, and if it isn't Saint Andrew himself, wrapped in his banner of righteousness and carrying his sword of truth."

"What are you talking about, man? And who gave you leave to make free with my kitchen? I'm in the habit of receiving guests in the parlor." Grandfather stood just inside the door. Even his beard frowned.

"Now, don't take on so, sir. It's myself that tempted him in for a nice bit of cake. Near perishing with hunger as he was." The motherly Mrs. Berkley intervened from her position in front of the Robinson stove. Although she was younger than her employer, she mothered him right along with the youngsters. Now she picked up a wheat bap chock-full of currants and nuts and handed it to the lord of the manor. "Now, you be telling me, sir. Would a plate of these be suiting you for your tea?"

Grandfather maintained his air of offended dignity, but he took the currant bun. "They will do nicely, Mrs. B." He gave the young men a severe look. "Berkley will serve us when we have all washed."

"Uncle, you oughtn't be so hard on the excellent Mrs. B," Thomas said a short time later. They were gathered around the dining room table. A low fire crackled on the grate, taking the nip off the September air. "We'd be happy enough to have her and her good husband at Price Manor. Our Iris is a good enough hand with the pies and puddings, but you do have a treasure here." He took a bite of his third currant bun. "And Berkley could buttle for Lord Londonderry himself."

"Don't talk such rot, Thomas Price. And don't you be telling me how to handle my servants. Now what are you here about?"

Thomas flashed his ready smile, exhibiting an expanse of perfect white teeth. "I've come seeking my cousin's company on a venture."

Andrew raised his head with a jerk from the heaped serving of stewed hare he had been diligently working his way through. He paused with knife and fork poised over his plate. What was the unpredictable Tammis up to now?

"I'm off to Donegal next week. We need some new brood mares, if we're to make the most of that fine blood stallion my father bought last spring. Thought you might be wanting to improve your bloodlines as well, Uncle Lanark."

Only one thing could bring a brighter light to Jay Lanark's eyes than the Lanark land or an Orange march, and that was the Lanark stables. "Oh, aye? Your da has a line on some good fillies does he now?"

"No doubt you've heard talk of the fine offerings at the Rossheely Fair last spring."

Jay shook his head. "Fat lot of good that'll do. They all sold. What're you thinking, man?"

"I'm thinking that the word is, there are signs it'll be a hard winter. There's many a small breeder will be glad enough to clear out his stable a bit this fall." Thomas laid a finger aside his nose and tapped knowingly. "So, as I'll be making the trip anyway, I thought I'd just offer to share what promises to be a fine windfall and take young Andrew here along as well. The lad's good enough company."

Andrew held his breath. A journey the breadth of Ireland with Tammis? He could think of nothing he would like better. A vision of shining freedom rose before him— nearly a hundred miles between himself and the stifling walls and fields of Lanarks' Bawn. He opened his mouth to accept.

"Unthinkable. Andrew is needed here."

Thomas laughed, his cheeks glowing pink before the fire. "Oh, come now, Uncle Lanark. Surely not needed. Wanted, of course. But not indispensable here, surely."

"We'll be harvesting the tatties in a few weeks."

"Of course. All Ireland will be. Biggest crop we've ever taken in—everyone says so. But you aren't suggesting Andrew is needed for field labor? How many croppies from the clachan owe you service?"

The firelight emphasized the bones of Grandfather's face. "These will be Andrew's fields one day. He needs the practice of supervising."

"Oh, I see. You have my sympathy. I didna know." Thomas held a hand over his heart. "And here was me, thinking Carlan Dunleer was still overseeing for you. But if he's no… well, that's a sore loss, a sore loss, indeed."

Jay struck the table. "I'll not be mocked at my own table by a puppy. Well ye know that Andrew must learn to oversee the overseer. Besides, we're to start a new building project. Hope to have it most completed before harvest. We'll be needing new storage sheds for the tatties.

"Far better ye'd do to be about looking to the care of yer own fields and tending more to the Word of God. 'Look to the ant, thou sluggard; consider her ways, and be wise: Which having no guide, overseer, or ruler, Provideth her meat in the summer, and gathereth her food in the harvest.'"

Andrew wondered if the edge to Grandfather's voice was a warning to himself not to extend the argument, or if it was directed to Tammis and the Price family at large. Jay Lanark held no toleration for the Prices' wishy-washy Methodist ways. If Grandfather had his way about it, he would have as little truck with the Price Manor relations and their Arminian enthusiasms as he'd had with the Seaton Court Lanarks and their popery, before they moved to Dublin or wherever it was they had gone off to. Wherever it was, their going had Jay Lanark's blessing.

Andrew bit his lip and looked at his cousin in appeal. There was nothing to be gained by angering his grandfather further. If an approach to Jay Lanark's love of fine horseflesh left him unmoved, there was no hope. "When do you go, Tammis?" Andrew made no attempt to keep the longing out of his voice.

"Next week. The fair starts end of the month. Take my time traveling, see a bit of the country, I thought. Then get there in time to look all the stock over good."

Jay Lanark's face clearly showed what he thought of young men gallivanting about the country on pleasure trips when they could be at home building bigger barns.

A few days later, the builder summoned by Jay Lanark arrived, and Andrew dutifully followed along, listening to Grandfather describe his vision for enlarging house and outbuildings. What could the joy of riding across the green beauty of Ireland be compared to good solid stone and boards?

Andrew counted the months in his head. No, counting months made it seem too many. He would stick with years. Four years and two months until he was of age. Then his mother's inheritance would come to him, and he would be independent.

But he couldn't wait that long for a breath of fresh air. No one could go for more than four years without breathing. Tammis would be leaving in a few days. Andrew felt desperate to find a way to accompany him. But what could he do? He didn't have two shillings of his own. And he wouldn't—couldn't—openly defy his grandfather. All he could do was hope for a miracle.

And obey. For the moment that meant saddling

Rannock while Grandfather left the builder with Carlan Dunleer to work out the details. Grandfather would then be ready to inspect the fields—if they could even see them through the mist that was rising thicker all the time. Andrew couldn't remember when they'd had such a cool, rainy summer—even in a land that seldom had anything but cool, rainy weather.

When he entered the stable, the young O'Brien met him with his usual liveliness. "You'll be wanting your horses now? I just gave Rannock a fine brushing. He's a beauty, he is. Best in the stable, I'm thinking."

Andrew let the lad chatter until a direct question required an answer.

"Then what's Joe Maguire about? You'll be having some building, then?"

"Aye. New barn. Room on the house." Andrew usually enjoyed chatting with Conor. Today he answered without thought.

But Conor jumped at the news. "Oh, that's grand. How many men can he be using? Me da, our Paddy, Uncle Des… I'll tell them. They'll be here in the morning. They can start the clearing away right off."

The lad's enthusiasm cut through Andrew's abstraction. He had not considered what the news of possible employment might mean in the clachan, and sure it was there was little enough to do on the land until time to harvest the potatoes next month.

"I'll be asking Mr. Dunleer, right enough," Conor concluded without waiting for an answer.

Andrew was in a slightly better mood a short time later when he rode out of the yard a few paces behind Grandfather. It even seemed the mist had lifted some.

They had just turned onto the lane leading to Scrabo Road when a carriage pulled by a fine team of matched grays came alongside and stopped.

The driver, a man with a fringe of brown beard and a well-groomed mustache, raised his high-crowned beaver hat. "Good day to you, gentlemen, and what a happy chance this is to be meeting our new neighbors. Harrowby's the name. Gordon Harrowby. Just settling into the place down the road. You'll know it as Seaton Court, but we're thinking of calling it Harrowby's Dale."

He laughed at their blank looks. "We're from Yorkshire, you see. From the dales. It'll remind us of home, like. But of course, as I tell the wife, this is our home now. Fine land here. Fine. The dales are good enow for grazing, but this is crop-growing land. Fine." Gordon Harrowby tipped his handsome gray hat in their direction.

Jay Lanark rode toward him, tipped his own hat, and introduced himself and his grandson.

Harrowby then presented his wife, Ellen, a plump blonde woman wearing a fringed black cape and black striped gown. She murmured something pleasant about the attractiveness of the neighborhood.

But to Andrew the time seemed endless until Mr. Harrowby got around to introducing the two young ladies in the back seat of the carriage: his daughters, Wilma and Selma.

Andrew struggled to fix the memory in his mind so that he would be able to tell them apart the next time they met. For of a certain, they must meet again. Often. It did seem that the curls escaping around the brim of Selma's blue-ribboned bonnet were more golden than the dark brown ringlets brushing Wilma's shoulder.

The young ladies dimpled charmingly and giggled, lowering their eyes.

Andrew sat as if Rannock had taken root, when the carriage rolled on down the lane.

"Well, there you are now, lad. And what do you say to that? Eh?" Grandfather gave him a hearty clap on the shoulder. "Nay, you needn't be telling me what you think. It's plain as a pikestaff on your face." He slapped his thigh sharply, and the horses pricked up their ears. "Twins. Now that's my idea of good breeders. Two for the price of one. You look sharp, young man. Just what this family needs. Too many puny women. Whole family getting weak." He squinted at his slimly built grandson. "Yes sir, need to thicken up the blood." He prodded his horse toward the closest field. "Yorkshire. Hm. Well, that's England, of course, but far enough from London—they should do all right."

Andrew let Grandfather's words wash over him as he savored the memory of dancing eyes and flickering dimples framed by the round brim of a straw bonnet. Sometimes the bonnet wore blue ribbons and sometimes green rosettes, but both were charming.

When they got to the first field, he was so lost in his

daydream that he had to blink three times to be sure he wasn't imagining the sight before him. Were those potato leaves, which had been so healthy three days ago, really covered with brownish black splotches? One look at Grandfather's face was surer confirmation than anything he saw in the field.

"What is it, Grandfather?"

Jay dismounted and knelt by the nearest plant, cupping it in his hands as a man might hold the face of his beloved. He moved on to the next hill. There he pulled the plant up. The roots were as rotted as the leaves. "I've never seen anything like it."

Andrew left his mount and knelt by his grandfather. "Is the whole field gone?"

Grandfather's speechlessness was more alarming than the ominous splotches on the potato leaves.

Jay pulled up another plant. That one had a few damaged leaves, but the tubers were sound. On further investigation, it appeared that about half the crop was lost. Completely rotted in less than three days.

"Doesn't look like we'll be needing the new store shed," Andrew said at last.

But Jay Lanark was descended from a long, hardy line. "Nonsense, boy. The very time to build. Locals will be needing employment. Besides—" he turned to the field behind them. "Did you ever see a finer stand of oats?"

· · ·

And so it was across the land. Strange black spots appeared overnight, withering more than half the potato crop. But there was no reason for alarm, people said. The potato crop had failed before, they said. Just ten years ago there had been widespread losses all across Ulster. And again in '37. But everyone had recouped the next year. No need for alarm.

Besides, the oats crop was the best anyone had seen for ten years. And Jay Lanark congratulated himself on his fine new storage barn that would keep the harvest safely dry until he could get the best price for it.

"Yes sir, couldn't have come at a better time. England's paying top money for oats this year." He surveyed the foundations that had just been laid for the new room on the house—his long gallery. "I heard of a Raeburn going for sale in Belfast. I just might make a start on my collection if I turn enough profit on these oats. Here, now, lad, it's a good time to be neighborly. Mrs. B made pear butter today. You ask her for a jar or two and take it to the Harrowbys to welcome them like."

Andrew jumped to his feet. That was not an order he needed to hear more than once.

"And you tell them not to be worrying. No need to worry. Any losses this year can more than be made up for next year. Nothing to worry about."

CHAPTER TWO

The next summer, Andrew would consider how prophetic Jay Lanark's words had been.

There had been empty stomachs in many a cottier's hut last winter. Infants had cried at their mother's breasts. Old women, huddling by the turf fire in their black shawls, had inched closer to the grave as the flesh thinned on their old bones. Many a tattie that should have been saved to seed the hillocks on Good Friday had been eaten to keep hunger beyond the doorstep.

But most had survived, and the gray, hungry days were all but forgotten now as fields flourished verdant and vigorous across the island. Everyone's spirits were buoyed by the prospect of an abundant harvest.

And although the croppies, who were never long out from under the shadow of starvation, called these the blue months—the time when winter stores were thin and harvest still a long wait—yet there were pleasures for cottier and landholder alike. And for Andrew that meant the Ballymena Fair. He smiled at the thought of spending the day with Wilma of the brown ringlets. And with the golden Selma. And their parents too, of course, he added hurriedly.

Oh, but Wilma, now… The attractions stacked up one upon another as Rannock's hooves plodded down the lane to Harrowby's Dale. He would buy her gingerbread and rock, and they would watch the boys run footraces, and admire the fine sheep and goats and finer still horses, and the travelers would be there with their brightly painted wagons, and there would be music around the campfires, and dancing in the street, and…

He turned into the tree-lined yard of the place he still thought of as Seaton Court, admiring the tall, colorful hollyhocks and spikes of lupine and delphinium growing around its whitewashed walls. Fresh gravel covered the open area between house and barns. Gordon Harrowby was a careful man indeed. A man who would be even more careful of his daughters than of his property.

Andrew sat tall in his saddle and endeavored to look reliable as he approached.

Thank goodness Grandfather had made the arrangements for the Lanarks to introduce their neighbors to the best fair in County Antrim. Andrew doubted his own courage in broaching the plan—or Mr. Harrowby's willingness to accept. But no one was likely to refuse Jay Lanark anything.

Andrew looked around at the sound of another horse

entering the yard. He hadn't expected Grandfather to arrive so soon, since, of course, he must ride around at least the closer of his fields before setting off on the day's outing.

In fact, it wasn't Jay Lanark but a dark-haired rider on a long-legged black stallion.

"Ah, Tammis! A fine thing to see you after these many months." The sight of his cousin brought back the painful memory of last fall's disappointment, though. "And did you have a fine adventure in Donegal?"

Thomas threw back his head and laughed in his open way. "And have we had so little communication these past months? I'd not realized you didn't know. I didna go, man."

Andrew frowned. "Didn't go?"

Thomas shook his head. "The crop failure. Too expensive to keep the beasts without potatoes to feed 'em. But it's just as well. With the fine crop this year—" he gestured as if exhibiting a flourishing potato field "—we'll have more than enough for an expanded stable. And last year's shortages will make the prices on horseflesh even better." He tapped the side of his nose and laughed again. "Fancy there'll be some pretty pickings at Ballymena."

Andrew had not known their party had been expanded, but he was glad enough for his cousin's presence, even if Grandfather wouldn't be.

A red-haired serving girl opened the door at Andrew's knock. Another O'Brien from the clachan, no doubt. She bobbed a curtsey and skittered off to call her mistress.

A moment later Mrs. Harrowby bustled into the hall. The wide lace bertha on her blue dress framed flushed cheeks, and her forehead creased in concern. At the sight of the gentleman callers she threw up her hands. "Oh dear, oh dear, oh dear. Here we are ready to go, and where are those girls? I can't keep up with them for two minutes together." She spun around with a swish of crinoline. "Mr. Harrowby! Where are you, husband? You must come and take charge of your daughters."

Then remembering her guests she turned back. "Do forgive me, gentlemen. Please." She gestured toward a sitting room opening off the hall. "Please, do take a seat. I'm certain they won't delay you long. Now where are those bothersome girls?" She turned back to the door before Andrew and Thomas were seated.

Gordon Harrowby entered in velvet-collared redingote and plaid trousers. "Tut, tut, don't fret yourself, woman. The lasses'll be along. Wilma found a bird caught in the hedge. Thinks it's injured its wing."

Andrew relaxed, glad to know she wasn't just avoiding him. "Oh, where is she, sir? Perhaps I could be of assistance."

"Oh, aye? Out back, then." Mr. Harrowby tipped his head in the direction of the door he had just come through.

Andrew found Wilma on her knees under a tree, a little brown bird cupped in her gloved hands.

She looked up with a small smile. "I'm sorry, Andrew. I can't go to the fair. This poor wee thing's hurt."

Andrew knelt beside her. "Is its wing broken?"

"I can't tell. But it can't fly. It'll die if I leave it."

Andrew felt carefully along the bone of the small wing

fanned over Wilma's hand. "I don't think it's broken. I could splint it just in case, but it's probably best just to let it rest. It'll need a dish of water. Where can we put it that the cats can't get to it?"

Wilma thought a moment. "In the henhouse."

"Right." Andrew got to his feet and helped her stand, an act requiring assistance as both her hands were full and her voluminous skirt and petticoats were tangled under her. In a few minutes, however, the wren was safely ensconced in an empty chicken nest. "There now, mission of mercy accomplished. We can go to the fair."

"Oh, not yet, Andrew. I must feed my bunnies." She set to pulling clover from beneath the hedgerow.

Andrew tried to hide his impatience. They would miss half the fun if this kept up much longer. "Can't rabbits do this for themselves?"

"No, these are just wee. I still give them milk too. Their mother was killed in a fearful trap. I searched and searched and was just lucky to find their nest under the roots of the big cottonwood, or they'd all have perished, the dearlings."

Andrew dutifully gave a hand with the bunnies. Then he waited while Wilma checked on a mongrel dog with a sore paw. In spite of his impatience, he did admire her skill with the creatures.

When they rounded the side of the house, Andrew saw that Grandfather had arrived. He did hope their tardiness would not produce too sharp a remark from the old man.

But they were fortunate in their timing. They went in one door just as Selma entered from the garden, her arms full of yellow and blue flowers, her cheeks flushed, a long white apron over her full gingham skirt, and her broad-brimmed gardening hat pushed back on her head. Andrew thought her one of the most enchanting sights he had ever seen. When he glanced at Thomas, he knew his cousin thought so, too. The amazing thing was Grandfather's almost courtly manner as he bowed to the young woman, brushing her hand with his beard.

Thus it was that the party set out in good humor, no matter how tardily, to Ballymena. Mr. Harrowby drove the ladies in the carriage while Jay, Andrew, and Thomas rode escort.

The village of Ballymena, a few miles north of Belfast, nestled in a green glen. Emerald hills clustered around it on every side. They were still some distance from the town when they began to see the barrel-hooped wagons of the "travelers"—red, yellow, pink, green—lining the verge of the road. Some had camped in fields. Flame-haired, green-eyed children, chickens, and scraggly dogs played in the hedgerows and around the wagon ponies' legs. Mothers and older sisters scolded them—children and animals alike—in a strange-sounding language.

Andrew smiled. This was hardly the great escape to the west country he had dreamed of last year, but it was a grand day out, and he never tired of the exhilaration of a fair.

Several tinkers had set up their metalworking trade

around the edge of the village. Anvils rang to the sound of hammered iron as horses were fitted with new shoes, cooking pots with new bottoms, and knife handles with new blades.

The visitors stabled their horses and set out. The sounds of penny whistles, fiddles, and bagpipes filled the air with a grand cacophony that had even Grandfather Lanark's toe tapping.

"Rock. Ballymena rock!" A green-eyed girl carrying a tray strapped around her shoulders called her wares.

In a moment Andrew had presented the Harrowby party with long sticks of crunchy, pink-and-white-striped candy.

But Grandfather would not put up with such dillydallying. He cut a straight line through the crowded village to the green, where a wide circle of observers and bidders scrutinized the horses offered for sale. As skilled as the travelers were in metalworking—some said their line went back to the fifth century when itinerate metalsmiths wandered the Irish countryside from the rath of one chieftain to the next—they were even more skilled at horse-trading. In fact, they were so skilled that few of the settled residents would bid for themselves.

Grandfather, however, shook his bush-like beard and raised a hand in refusal as a sandy-bearded man in a tall tweed hat approached him. Jay Lanark would as soon implore a saint to intercede for him with the Almighty as he would employ an agent to do his horse dealing.

It was easy to see that Andrew's grandfather had his eye

on a very special animal. Andrew saw instantly what a fine addition the little red mare would make to the Lanarks' Bawn stable. And after Jay had looked her over carefully, there was even less room to doubt her suitability.

The tinker showing her held her lead rope loosely and walked her around the ring in both directions. Then, lengthening the rope to give her more headroom, he ran her around at a brisk trot.

Lanarks' Bawn had long produced fine pleasure horses. And now, as the little mare showed her smooth-gaited action and Andrew coupled her in his mind with the long-legged, fiery stallion that was their prize breeder, he could see Grandfather determining to breed horses the rival of Lord Londonderry's.

But his grandfather walked off, shaking his head. "Too delicate. You'd be lucky if she survived her first foaling," he said loudly. He didn't go far away from the circle, though—just to the other side, where he seemingly gave all his attention to a small black cart pony, which he urged Gordon Harrowby to consider for his daughters.

Selma clapped her hands at the idea. "Oh, what a fine thing, Father. I would love to drive a pony cart. I always wanted one in Yorkshire, but it would be even lovelier here for exploring the countryside."

Andrew tugged at his grandfather's coat. The bidding had begun on the red mare.

Jay Lanark hung back. No need to come in at the early stages. Let the others run themselves out. He would know the strategic moment to enter the proceedings. No doubt he had calculated the value of the animal to a fair penny. He also knew many of the interested breeders around the ring and had an equally shrewd knowledge of the depth of their pockets.

The only thing Grandfather obviously hadn't calculated was the wit and quickness of the agents—the "guinea hunters." They bid sometimes in English, sometimes in their strange, coded language, but always with an insouciant skill that was unsettling to one who believed everything in life could be approached with commonsense logic. Jay's one offer was lost in the shuffle. The mare went home with a rival breeder from Bangor who had previously sold three colts to Lord Londonderry.

Andrew turned to offer his arm to Wilma, as much to escape his grandfather's displeasure as in anticipation of enjoying the lively reel he heard coming from the other side of a wagon. But it was not Wilma at his elbow. Rather, he turned toward the sandy bush of the guinea man who had earlier been rebuffed by his grandfather. "Fancy yon mare, did ye?"

Andrew raised his eyebrows and shrugged. "Nice animal. A mite small, but nice."

The traveler winked, nodded, and tapped the side of his nose. "Aye. I know where there's a whole stable like that. And better."

"Of the same stock?"

Andrew started at Thomas' question. He hadn't seen his cousin approach.

"Aye. The same."

It was not for nothing that the genius horse traders of the traveling folk were called guinea hunters. A flash of gold passed between Thomas and the man's hand. It as quickly disappeared into the pocket of his flowered waistcoat. "They'll be at the Rossheely Fair, first week in August."

Thomas clapped his arm around the fellow's shoulders. "I know the very place. To the west above Sligo Bay. Near the Donegal border."

"Aye. That's the one. Best in all Ireland."

"So I've heard." Thomas gave the man a shrewd look. "You'll not be forgetting me, now, my friend?"

The tinker patted his pocket where Thomas' guinea lay. "Travelers have long memories. And don't forget me. Gabriel's the name—like the angel." He gave a twinkling grin before melting into the circle surrounding the horse ring.

The music from across the field was livelier than before. Now was Andrew's opportunity for the dance he had been anticipating ever since plans for the day had been laid. But Wilma was nowhere to be seen. He would gladly have asked Selma to join the reel with him, but his cousin's intentions in that direction were too clear.

"Where has your sister got off to now?" Andrew's question to Selma held a note of irritation.

She pointed to the far side of the field where stood a bright green wagon embellished with yellow scrollwork and red flowers.

Andrew could see Gordon Harrowby's back but not the

man's daughter. As Andrew approached the small group by the caravan, however, he spotted the lady. As usual, she was on her knees beside a distressed animal. Andrew sighed as he saw Tammis lead Selma toward the set forming a new square for the reel.

Wilma lifted the colt's right forehoof and turned to the child standing beside her and sucking a grimy finger while tears streaked trails down her cheeks. "See there—your pony has a stone in his frog."

The girl's round green eyes grew rounder still at the seemingly incomprehensible words. A boy a year or two older pressed forward.

Andrew picked up a small, sturdy stick and handed it to Wilma.

In a moment her prodding dislodged the stone. "Your pony may still limp for a day or two. The stone may have bruised the tender place, but he'll be all right."

"Here now, lady, sure and don't you be sporting with my sister. I'm after knowing that's no frog."

Wilma smiled and picked up the hoof again, bending it so the young lad could see the underside. She tapped the soft, black formation. "See, that's called a frog. It looks like he stepped on a nice, fat frog and it stuck there, doesn't it?" She set the foot down and stood with Andrew's assistance, brushing bits of grass from her skirt. "And next time don't you be making fun of your little sister when she's worried about a hurt animal."

She explained to Andrew as she took his arm. "The older boys and girls were tormenting her for crying over the limping pony. But she stood right up to children twice her size."

"And you came along and rescued them all." Andrew smiled at his fair friend.

"It's lucky that Father and I were walking this way. The stone might have worked itself in much deeper if it hadn't been removed quickly."

"And it never occurred to you to let one of the tinkers deal with it—or even your father—or myself?"

She looked at him with eyes as wide and green as those of the tinker child. "But I got there first. And I did it perfectly. With your stick. Thank you—it was just right."

He opened his mouth to ask her to join the set for the next reel, but now Mrs. Harrowby approached. "My dears, there you all are. I'm sure I was quite convinced that you'd been stolen by the gypsies."

Andrew started to explain that Irish travelers were an entirely different people from the nomadic Romany. But Mrs. Harrowby would have known that, and there was no convincing the good lady that it wasn't quite time for them to return home—especially as a rather heavy rain had started to fall.

By the time they reached Lanarks' Bawn, Andrew was in a thorough funk. He was wet through and chilled to the bone. He had given his coat to Mrs. Harrowby when it was obvious that the cover on the carriage was insufficient to protect its passengers from the rain and wind. He had had nothing but a stick of Ballymena rock to eat for the space of several hours. He had not had his hoped-for dance with

Wilma, who obviously preferred injured animals to his company. And Grandfather had failed to buy the mare he wanted. How could so many things go wrong in one day?

He flung off his drenched waistcoat and threw himself into a chair before the blazing peat fire Berkley had ready for them. Grandfather entered more deliberately, and Andrew held his breath. All he needed to end the day was a lecture. What had he done wrong now? he wondered. Oh well, he would soon know.

"Andrew, I've made a decision. And I'll brook no argument. I mean to be obeyed in this."

Andrew sighed and ran his fingers through his dripping hair.

"Thomas told me about the fair at Rossheely. I shall have my new mare. I would go myself, but you aren't ready to take charge of the fields."

Andrew choked.

Grandfather cut him off with a wave. "Don't interrupt, boy. You'll go to the fair and buy a mare for me. The best mare in all Ireland, do you hear? I'll not be crossed in this."

Andrew was so dumbfounded that it seemed a full minute before he could manage a weak, "Yes, Grandfather."

CHAPTER THREE

ndrew's appetite to see more, to travel farther, amused his cousin. "Aye, Andrew, laddie, hunger for adventure's a fine thing. But not when ye put it before filling your stomach."

Andrew grinned. He was always ready to eat. "Right. We'll stop wherever you say. Under that tree ahead, maybe? But Tammis, I'd no idea the land is so grand. I knew seeing it would be fine, but Lough Neagh is near the size of the sea!"

Even through the mist enveloping land and riders, the low, marshy surrounds of the lough were visible. Two large waterfowl flew by, their rasping call drawing replies from nests among the reeds and grasses.

Thomas swatted at a buzz of midges. "Aye, it is more of an inland sea. But is this truly your first time away from Lanarks' Bawn?"

Andrew drew in a deep breath. "Aye, for any great time or distance without Grandfather."

Thomas gave a shout of laughter. "You're a sturdy lad, Andrew Armstrong, a sturdy lad. Living with your grandfather. My mother, God rest her soul, used to say, 'That man is so rigid I'm surprised he can bend his knees to sit in a chair.' But then, we're promised that tribulation worketh patience. Maybe that's why I'm so impatient—not enough tribulation."

But even Thomas' impatient stomach had to wait longer. By the time they reached the beech tree, rain was falling beyond the ability of its thick leaves to shelter travelers. And it was almost a mile farther along before they found a rocky outcrop with sufficient overhang to offer protection.

Mrs. Berkley had left nothing to chance in preparing for the young master's journey. Andrew pulled a loaf of brack, a boiled chicken, and a small, round cheese from his saddlebags. "Don't bother opening yours, Tammis. There's more than enough here for two—even with your appetite."

Thomas pulled a jug of cider from his pack. "Aye. Hunger is a bad thing, but thirst is worse."

They leaned against the rocky wall to enjoy their meal while the horses grazed along the bank of a stream.

"Well, there should be full stomachs in every cottage hereabouts come October." Andrew gestured to the fields before them. Potato plants spread broad leaves over every ridge and extended down into the furrows as well. Such vigorous top growth gave promise of fine, firm-fleshed tubers growing thick under the brown earth. This year, little space around the edges of the fields had been given to growing oats and wheat. Cash crops were a luxury. Potatoes were the thin line of existence for man and beast. And after last year's widespread crop failure, there was even less margin for survival than usual.

Thomas nodded. "Aye. A good thing the promise is prosperous. The blue months have been bad for the croppies this year."

Andrew chewed a mouthful of crusty wheat loaf stuffed with currants and paused to ponder. His vittles had always appeared as if by magic on the table on schedule. He had never before given the matter consideration. "What do they do? When there're no tatties?"

"Those that can, go over the water to work. Some scrutch flax for landlords here. Those with wracking rights —like the cottiers along Strangford—pick the shellfish out of the seaweed. Some of the kelp's edible, too."

Andrew made a face. "Urgh! Have you ever smelled that stuff? Bad enough when they manure the fields with it. Can't imagine eating it." No wonder, then, that Conor O'Brien had been so eager to secure work for his cousins and uncles.

He sank his teeth into a chicken leg. After a few moments of chewing in rhythm with the sound of rain dripping from the ledge overhead, he asked, "Will we go to Armagh? I hear it's a fine city."

Thomas nodded. "It is that. But out of our way. We'll find an inn near Craigavon before dark."

"But we've no hurry, have we? We could go tomorrow."

Thomas' laughter echoed inside their rocky shelter. "Oh, aye. And while we're at it, we'll just nip on down to Dublin. And maybe you'd fancy seeing Cork? Or taking a wee run over to London? It's little wonder Jay Lanark kept you on a short lead. We've horses to buy, man!"

Tammis put a wedge of cheese back into its cloth and stood up. "Afterwards…" He gave his young cousin a wink. "We'll be for seeing what might develop. But we'd best be getting on down the road now if we don't want to be spending the night under a dripping rock."

Whatever Tammis had in mind, he apparently didn't want to talk about it yet. But there was plenty to occupy Andrew as they carried on westward. His mind had been held captive by the narrow world of the Bawn. Now that he was beyond it, his new freedom gave his thoughts scope for roaming, just as his eyes were able to do. The wider vistas gave rise to thoughts of what might lie beyond—beyond the next hill, even beyond this life. The few sermons he had managed to pay attention to in meeting had once satisfied any curiosity he might have felt about matters of infinity. But now he wondered. "What do you think about it all, Tammis?"

"All what?"

Andrew shrugged. "Creation. God. All that."

Thomas was quiet for a while. He gazed around in every direction, then looked upward as if trying to see beyond the clouds. "Oh, I reckon the Almighty's up there.

Not sure what He's doing, though. Don't think about it much."

Andrew nodded. "Me neither." Mostly he had avoided such questions, for whenever Andrew thought of God, a picture of Jay Lanark's face came to him. And if the Almighty was as rigid as Grandfather, Andrew could see little use in religion. He didn't need another set of rules. But sometimes one did wonder.

It was after noon five days later when they passed their first red tinker's wagon and knew they were nearing their goal. The only room to be had in town was a small, dark hole upstairs at the public house. It smelled of must and stale smoke, and the husk-filled mattress was lumpy and damp. But they were glad for it. And, Andrew thought, they'd be spending little enough time in it anyway.

The opening day of the fair was called "gathering day" because the travelers from far and wide made special effort to gather here at the liveliest horse fair in Ireland.

The cousins had no more than finished their morning porridge when they heard a great stirring in the street. Pipes, drums and whistles, shouts, calls, and laughter combined to bring them running from the inn into High Street. There a fine procession greeted them. The street was jammed with about equal parts viewers, paraders, and children with pets running alongside.

At the center of all the hoopla was the largest, shaggiest goat Andrew had ever seen. His grand curving horns spanned at least three feet, and bright ribbons streamed from horns and hair alike. Red-haired, barefoot girls in whirling skirts skipped and danced before the creature, clapping their hands and strewing the path with flowers.

"*Rí Síogaí*!" The shout went up wherever the goat passed, chewing placidly on a mouthful of daisies.

Andrew was thoroughly bewildered, but Thomas shouted and cheered with the others. "What's it all about?" Andrew asked as the commotion passed on down the street.

"The fairy king. King of the fair."

"A goat?"

Tammis shrugged. "Something about a goat giving warning to the sleeping town when their enemies were attacking."

They joined the crowd accompanying the procession. "How do you know so much about all this?"

"Grew up listening to my great-aunt's tales. She lived with us after her husband died. I adored her. She could tell tales to outdo any *seanchaidh*. She had married a Methodist preacher. They traveled all over the island, holding meetings." Tammis' cheerful face was soft with remembrance. "Aye, Auntie Carolenn knew everything. And hearing her tell about it was as good as being there."

Andrew kept trying to remind himself that they were here on business. There were horses to be evaluated, bargains to be sized up and argued over, deals to be struck. He daren't return to Lanarks' Bawn without the best broodmare that ever graced Irish soil. But it was hard to keep one's mind on business when there were so many distractions.

Tammis seemed unusually drawn to the musicians who filled every nook of High Street and meadow with lilting tunes.

Surprisingly, it wasn't the livelier pipes and fiddles that attracted him most but the gentler harpers and the lone singers. Thomas could even be in the midst of inspecting a likely piece of horseflesh and break off to talk briefly to a passing musician.

Andrew bought a large square of spicy, warm gingerbread for a penny and wandered down a winding lane where barkers vied with one another to lure passers-by to games of chance. He risked a farthing on the proposition that he could point out which of three walnut shells had the stone under it. He was certain he had not taken his eye from the correct one. But when he pointed to the shell in the middle, it was empty.

He shrugged and walked on. Sellers offered trays of ribbons, pins, polished shells, every geegaw imaginable. A little girl offered straw St. Bridget's crosses for a ha'penny. An old woman with three teeth missing called out to passers to buy her Celtic crosses, "Pure gold as the living sun, and blessed by Saint Patrick himself."

Andrew paused.

"Sure and you'll be wanting one to give to your lassie. You'd not go home without a fairing for her, would you, now?"

Andrew smiled and looked over the tray. The woman's

words were true enough. For all the fun and excitement, an awareness of the fair's missing element had been growing on him all day. Wilma Harrowby was the width of Ireland away from him. Rossheely Fair was maybe three times the size and merriment of Ballymena, yet without Wilma's company it lacked luster. And the street dancing held no attraction at all.

He paused over a tray of ribbons and beads, thinking how fine the emerald satin bows would look holding Wilma's shining ringlets.

But he hesitated. He mustn't spend all his money until the horse-dealing was done. It wouldn't do to be outbid because he had spent his purse on fairings. Reluctantly, he shook his head and strolled on a few paces. He paused to watch a juggler, then started back toward the horse meadow.

He had just caught sight of Tammis and was hurrying toward him when the clear, pure trill from a harp stopped him dead in his tracks. It sounded like the warble of a lark amid a cacophony of crows.

Andrew followed the sound to where a thin old man in a faded green jacket sat caressing a harp of highly polished black bog oak. A length of canvas provided a sort of shelter from the intermittent rain. A large brindled dog lay at his feet. Children raced by, adults passed laughing and talking, donkeys brayed, sheep bleated, but the ancient musician— wispy white hair falling to his shoulders, and skin as thin and pale as paper stretched tight over his high cheekbones —seemed unaware of anything but his music.

The small bowl beside his chair contained only two farthings and a ha'penny, but the otherworldly appearance of the man and the angelic sound of the harp gave the impression that he had little need for anything as mundane as money. Just the same, Andrew tossed a groat in the bowl, not even thinking about horse-dealing or what the absence of a fourpenny piece might do to his bargaining capacity.

The tune went on for a long time, as if the player's fingers were singing repeated verses in his head, each with a slight variation. But at last, the melody ended on a rising glissando, and the air fluttered off on butterfly wings. Andrew stood barely breathing as the harper's fingers stilled on the strings.

Then a young girl, perhaps fourteen—no more than sixteen, certain—came from behind the tent. She took the harp gently from the frail hands and replaced it with a steaming beaker. "Here, now, *Seanathair*, I've a fine mussel stew for you. Drink ye all of it. It'll keep the chill out."

"Aye, you've my thanks. You're good to me, child."

Andrew saw then that the old man was blind. But his granddaughter's eyes were wide and round, and even from where Andrew stood, he could see they were bright as emeralds. And her cloud of red-gold hair was a light in the overcast day. She glanced at the silver coin among the coppers, then at Andrew, and flashed him a smile. He turned reluctantly to the horse ring.

•　•　•

The Thomas Andrew now encountered was a different person from the carefree companion who had laughed his way across Ireland. Now he was all business. He sized up every horse in the field and asked sharply judged questions of all the other men who were standing around, likewise examining the prospects.

Andrew considered how strange it was that the easy-going Tammis was suddenly so focused, while Andrew himself, usually so intense, was romping about the fair like a child. But little matter how childlike he might feel. He had a job to do, and he couldn't leave it all to his cousin.

"What have you seen, Tammis? Anything worth bidding on?"

"Oh, decided to look at the horses, did you? Thought I'd seen the back of you for good. Thought maybe you'd run off and joined the travelers."

"Just looking around, Tammis. But I'll settle now."

"Eh, well. Then you might take a look at the little filly over there. A first cousin to the one your grandfather wanted at Ballymena—if not a sister."

Andrew walked around her, not letting his interest show too clearly. "Aye, she is. Only better developed in the hindquarters. Should breed good." Grandfather had taught him what to look for in horses as well as in women. The two cousins turned away from the ring.

Behind them a pelter of bidding rang out as a little cart pony was run around the ring by his handler. The showing and bidding would go on all day. This was only the opening. The serious buying would begin tomorrow. Then they would need their guinea man. But the sandy-bearded Gabriel, he of the tweed stovepipe hat, was not to be found.

"You'll never see his shadow again," Andrew said over their pot of greasy lamb stew at the inn that night. "Probably got so roaring drunk on your gold that the whole thing went right out of his head."

Thomas bellowed the easy laughter that had returned when he left the business side of the horse fair. "Sometimes I could swear I hear Jay Lanark speaking out of your mouth, cousin."

Andrew's brown eyes flashed. He hit the table to chase away the image of Grandfather. *A true Lanark at heart, just like me.* "No. I'm nothing like my grandfather."

Thomas held up his hands. "Whoa, easy. I'd no mind to anger you, man."

But Andrew wondered. The last thing in the world he wanted was to grow up narrow and rigid like Grandfather Lanark. But was it happening anyway, in spite of his determination to get away from all the legalism that inhabited the bawn? "No. Grandfather would never have given a coin to a harper." And tomorrow he would go back and buy those ribbons for Wilma.

Thomas was instantly all attention. "Harper? I saw no harper worth tossing a coin to. Just an endless procession of tooting whistles, caterwauling pipes, screeching fiddles, and banging bodhran." He shook his head. "I think you must have dreamed your harper as an escape from the clamor."

"Nay, not a bit of it." And Andrew told him in detail

about the musician and his granddaughter.

"Aye." Thomas nodded. "Now I understand the sudden liking for the harp."

Andrew smiled. The day had been all that the grand gathering of the Rossheely Fair should have been. But tomorrow would be different, he promised himself. Tomorrow he would attend to the business of the little red mare with the finely rounded rump. He would bid as skillfully as any guinea hunter. He'd seen it done. He knew what to do. And for once Grandfather Lanark would be proud of him.

The next day he saw that the crowd at the horse ring had at least doubled, both in the number of animals being offered and in prospective buyers.

Andrew held true to his determination. In spite of a gnawing in his stomach for a tasty bit of gingerbread—and several fleeting thoughts of listening to harp music and gazing at emerald eyes—he examined every mare as thoroughly as Grandfather himself would have done. And at the end of it all he was satisfied that the little red filly was the one for Lanarks' stable. He had already named her —Fairling.

Throughout the morning, Thomas had bid on several beasts, but Andrew knew his cousin was waiting for a certain chestnut mare to enter the circle.

And then he felt more than saw a flutter off to one side. A man in a flat tweed cap brought Fairling into the ring.

Remembering Grandfather's nonchalant stance at Bally-mena, he held back, just on the edge of the inside circle, and let the bidding start. He had to judge the matter just right. If he tipped his hand and entered in too soon, he would just run his own price up and encourage others to go higher than he could afford. If he held off too long, he could have the bid stolen from under him as it had been with Grandfather—although now he was certainly glad that had been so.

In spite of the cool air, Andrew felt sweat break out at the back of his neck. What if he muffed the whole thing? Grandfather would never give him a second chance. The bidding crept up. He held his breath and again mentally counted the coins and pound notes in his pocket. What if the bidding surpassed his limit before he even had a chance to bid? Perhaps he could attempt to talk the winner into trading the filly for Rannock. Would Andrew have the heart to do that?

Then he realized that the bidding had slowed. The auctioneer in the middle of the ring cleared his throat. Andrew started to open his mouth.

But no sound emerged. A large, freckled hand with red hairs on the back clamped over Andrew's mouth and drew him backward into the crowd. He struggled. He tried to punch backward, but the larger man's grip held. It mattered little. The mare went to the last bidder.

Andrew's assailant spun him around and held him by the shoulders, just out of reach of the lad's spitting and kicking.

Then Andrew recognized the man through his blaze of fury. More accurately, he recognized the hat and beard. "What do you think you're doing? My cousin engaged you to help us! Is this the way you repay his generosity?"

"Aye, it is. I'm thinking you should know that mare was a twin. And the other one was born blind, a weakness this one could carry, too. You'll be wanting a proven broodmare, I'm thinking. I've found you a deal—two for the price of one."

He led the way beyond the field to a quiet corner where stood a bright green wagon painted with distinctive yellow scrollwork and red flowers. Andrew recognized it. Beside it, back in Ballymena, Wilma had cared for a pony's forefoot.

On the other side of the wagon stood a sleek, proud mare giving suck to a long-legged foal that couldn't be above a few hours old.

"See what I mean?" the guinea man said. "More interesting things elsewhere than the sale yard sometimes."

"Aye." Andrew had to admit mother and child were beauties. But it wasn't only the double value price that appealed to him. He was most struck by the fact that the mare's red-gold coat was the exact color of the harper's daughter's hair. He handed the agent another golden guinea.

"Leave it to me." The man ambled toward the wagon, stroking his bush of a beard.

There was nothing for Andrew to do there. Indeed, his presence would be a detriment. He nipped down a winding side street and bought the green ribbons for

Wilma. And now he had time to wonder about the harper. Was he even still here? And the emerald-eyed granddaughter. It was testimony to the intensity of Andrew's former work-centered concentration that this was the first thought he had given the matter since the bidding began.

But now that he'd left the noise of the sale ring, it wasn't long before his ears picked up the sweet note he was listening for. The length of canvas on poles, forming a tent roof and back, stood in the same place.

And there was Thomas, his head thrown back, laughing at something she of the red-gold hair had just said to him. Even the harper smiled at his cousin's infectious laughter. And the girl joined in like a chiming of golden bells. Andrew stood frowning.

Thomas turned and threw his arms wide. "Andrew Armstrong, the very lad. Come meet your Cousin Bridget!"

Andrew didn't move. Could even Thomas have worked that fast?

"Aye, man, I'd not told you, because the chances were so sparse, but I was determined that, if I ever got near to Donegal, I'd seek out the MacHenry relations Great-aunt Carolenn always told me about."

It was a long, involved tale. Some early Lanark daughter had run off, enchanted with a harper. It seemed that Carolenn Price had traced her ancestor with the aid of an acquaintance who traveled about collecting Irish melodies. Andrew couldn't follow the convolutions of the story, but all that mattered was the enchantment of listening to Bridget MacHenry's voice with the sounds of the *cláirseach* shimmering behind.

Andrew stood in tongue-tied fascination, while Thomas bantered easily with his new-found relation. The lackadaisical rain ceased and a full sun sparkled the crystal air, warming Andrew's head. He felt he could have stood in the magical moment forever. Perhaps he truly had entered the realm of the fairy king.

But the spell was broken soon enough. The men must needs turn to practical matters. For all that it was a bargain, the foal presented certain problems. Until its wobbly legs gained strength, it couldn't travel far in a day. It certainly couldn't get out of sight of its mother, or they would both go quite wild.

The next morning, Thomas returned triumphant from the sale ring with his white-footed chestnut mare. Once more the canny guinea man had struck a bargain that presented a happy solution. The traveler had convinced the mare's seller to include a soft leather saddle—which led Thomas to suggest that they might offer their newfound cousins a ride home.

The distance was short enough on horseback, even with a new foal following, but it amounted to a long walk for an ancient, blind harper. And Andrew had the pleasure of discovering that Bridget's eyes looked even more like cut gems when they were bright with gratitude.

So their return journey began with a northward detour.

The slim old man sat stiffly erect—his cherished black bogwood harp in a bag slung over his shoulder—atop Thomas' new mare, with his faithful, shaggy dog Madoo trotting at the horse's heels. Bridget rode bareback astride the foal's mother, her full green skirt pulled up to reveal slim white calves. Even though it was a matter of only a few miles, they stopped frequently to allow the foal, who now bore the name of Fairling, to suckle.

It was on the third of these pauses that Andrew looked out across a nearby potato field, and the sight chilled him. Something was wrong. Connacht was known for its thin, rocky soil. It produced crops poorer than any other in the island—that was why most of it was left to the native Irish. But this was something far worse than sparse growth. This was something sinister.

The potato leaves, which should have been broad and lush green, were curled and black-spotted. The blight had struck again.

Andrew's first instinct was to cry out, then he stopped himself. There was nothing to be gained by dismaying their guests. Bridget would surely see it soon enough for herself, but the old harper's comfort could be preserved for a time.

Andrew had no sooner conceived that convenient thought, however, than one glance at the wraith-like face— its thin nose held up to the air, a look of combined dismay and revulsion twisting the mouth—made him realize: Of course, the blind grandfather would be the first to smell the odor of rot that underlay what should have been spring-fresh air.

The little party that had set out in such high spirits arrived at the harper's cottage silent and tense. How bad was it? How widespread?

Last year, less than a third of the crop had survived. What would happen if this failure was as severe? It was beyond comprehension to consider that it might be worse. The Tory government had repealed the Corn Laws, allowing wheat and oats to flow into Ireland and be sold cheaply. But would this cheap, imported grain be adequate to feed a population formerly totally dependent on the potato for survival?

And then, a mile or so on, slowed by worry, they rounded a bend in the road and Andrew saw the harper's cottage. He had expected little. He found less. The one-room building was all of a piece with its surroundings. Its stone walls had been gathered from the earth on the spot where it stood. The timbers supporting its roof had been dug from the nearby bog. The roof thatch had been harvested from the fields, and its inside walls no doubt were blackened with the smoke of burning peat—likewise cut from the bog.

It appeared that Bridget, who had lived there all her life, saw it for the first time through the eyes of another. "I'm sorry. I didn't think. I was so happy for *Seanathair* to have a ride home. But it's all right. There's the lean-to. Dermot and I will sleep there. You can have our pallets. The brychans are warm."

Andrew was torn between asking who Dermot was and protesting that he wouldn't consider taking her sleeping place. But in truth, he was too stunned to speak. He merely nodded and entered the hut.

The floor was beaten earth. Turfs burning in the fireplace at the far end of the cottage filled the room with warmth—and with smoke. His eyes watered and his nose wrinkled at the foul, heavy sent of decayed earth. Andrew blinked to clear his eyes and gazed around the dimly lit room. Piles of straw covered with coarse-looking brychans along one wall indicated a sleeping place. A bare wooden table was to the right of the door and the room's single window opened over the table. An iron rush holder stood in the window. Could people truly *live* like this?

Bridget pulled a dried rush from a basket by the fireplace and lit one end. She stuck the other in the holder and motioned for their guests to take seats on the bench beside the fireplace. "Sit you down."

Andrew looked about desperately. What could he say? Then his eye lit on the straw weavings—one beside the door, one by the fireplace. "Oh, what fine crosses." Every cottage in the clachan had similar ones, but the intricacy of these was particularly skillful.

Bridget smiled. "The Bridget crosses? I'm after making them. They keep the evil out the door and the hearth safe from fire and ravagement."

She turned to Brendan MacHenry. "Now, *Seanathair*, you must give our guests a song while I boil the kettle." She placed the *cláirseach* in his hands and settled him on a stool.

The brindled Madoo nestled against the old man, who

stroked the dog's crisp hair before caressing the harp.

The moment his fingers touched the strings, the dark pushed back, chased into corners by silvery notes. Andrew felt warmed, his stomach less empty. It wasn't as bad here as the shock of first sight had led him to believe. After all, scores of people in the clachan back home lived this way. The cabin was snug against the weather—and the smell of burning peat was preferable to the odor of decay outdoors.

Thomas had given Bridget a full saddlebag to provide their supper—and many meals beyond their going. They would sleep well tonight. And tomorrow they would see that the blight was not so widespread. They would find it isolated to only a few fields, a shortage that could easily be made up for with imported corn.

Bridget sang to her grandfather's tune as she put oatcakes on the griddle to bake and held strips of bacon over the fire in a long-handled iron frame until the edges browned and curled. The fat sizzled as it fell on the hot peat bricks.

Andrew was just relaxing when the snug ambiance was shattered by the pounding of heavy blows. The wooden slab door trembled, then slammed against the stones of the fireplace. A hard-muscled young man about Andrew's age entered with a bellow. The abrupt shattering of the atmosphere was as if an angry bull had rampaged through the entrance. "And what are ye after doing, *Deirfiúr?*"

Andrew knew only a few words of Irish, but he realized that the angry young man—he must be the Dermot to whom Bridget had referred earlier—had called her sister.

"As ye can see if the drink has left you with eyes in your head, we've guests, *Deartháir*." She called him brother.

"Aye, and you'd drink, too, if you'd been in the fields these three days instead of off fairing." Dermot held a flat-bottomed wooden trug in his arms. He dumped its contents on the floor. The potatoes hit the hard earth with a sickening splat. The rancid stench that the air had only hinted at earlier filled the cottage.

"Go wash, Dermot. We've food for tonight, and you'll feel better with something solid inside." She scooped the rotten lumps back into the carrier and threw them out the door.

It was a tense, silent meal. Dermot took his plate to the corner and sat on a brychan. Bridget ate standing up, since the bench and stool were occupied.

Andrew cast about in his mind for something hopeful to say. "Seems Peel will have to send to America for more of their maize. That made up for last year's losses—surely it will see us through again." He felt a hypocrite before the words left his mouth. He had eaten no American maize. But Conor O'Brien had talked of the strange flat corn cakes his sister baked from the grain whose importation had been arranged by the English prime minister. And it had quickly become evident that the foreign grain was not as complete a food as the potato. Relying on it as the whole source of nutrition had resulted in violent outbreaks of scurvy and dysentery.

Dermot jumped to his feet and nigh split the table with his fist. "There'll be no more American maize. Or anything else. Where have ye been, man? It's all that's talked of in the dram shop. Peel's government fell. Lord Russell has vowed to stop all distribution of grain. No more subsidized food. With the potatoes rotting in the field again, that means no more food. Period." He banged out of the cabin as wildly as he had flung himself in.

Andrew looked around the dismal cottage, still reeking with the smell of rot. What would they do? The MacHenrys and the O'Briens and millions like them across the land? Life was hard enough at the best of times. Could they survive another winter without potatoes and with no subsidized grain? Months and months on boiled kelp and mussels—for those who could get them? He tried to think what he could do. He thought wildly of giving Bridget the mare and foal, then realized that would be a liability— more mouths to feed.

In the end he emptied his pockets of all but the few coins he would need for his return trip.

"I couldn't take it. It wouldn't be right. Charity—" She backed away from him.

"Not charity!" He spoke angrily, then cast about wildly in his mind. What could he say to convince her? "Not charity. Payment. Payment for—" *For what?* He glimpsed the harp in the corner by his stool. "Music. Payment for music..." He faltered, then he knew. "For your grandfather's music. When you've time, you must write it down. It's valuable. People will buy it—"

Her brittle laughter stopped him. This was not the golden bells he had heard from her before. "I can't."

"You can't write?"

"I can, then." Her chin lifted defiantly and her eyes flashed. Then she dropped her head and added, "A little." Head up again she concluded, "Father Lynch taught us at the hedge school. But I can't set down music."

He saw the problem, but he wouldn't give up. "You must learn the tunes then."

She looked from him to the coins in her hand and back to him once more. She nodded. "Come you back, then."

Andrew and Thomas left early the next morning, anxious to be gone before they stressed the meager household further. Besides, it would be slow going with the wobbly colt.

They were half a field away, Bridget still standing by the door waving, when Andrew turned Rannock and spurred back. In front of the cottage he drew up and shoved a hand into his pocket.

He pulled out the emerald satin ribbons and leaned toward her. "Here," he commanded almost harshly, and thrust them into her hand. "They match your eyes." He didn't look back as he galloped off.

And so began the nightmare trek across the land that less than a week before had been magically beautiful. Every mile they rode, it seemed the fields grew blacker and the atmosphere thicker with the stink of decomposition. By the time they reached home, the very air was brown with hunger.

CHAPTER FOUR

"The supply of the home market may safely be left to the foresight of private merchants'!" Andrew crumpled the *Northern Whig* and dashed it to the floor. "Supply of the home market! What home market? Has the man ever been to Ireland? What 'private corn' does he think there is here? Doesn't he realize these people have no money to buy his 'private corn' if it did exist?"

Jay Lanark crossed his feet propped on a stool before the fire. Outside, a howling wind rattled the windowpanes. "Don't get overheated, lad. And I'll thank you not to rumple my newspaper. Lord John Russell has the best economic advisers in the kingdom."

"Economic theory be—" Andrew strangled the word back at a warning look from his grandfather.

In spite of Andrew's agitation, Grandfather remained relaxed, stroking his ample beard. "If you'd calm down long enough to read what's left of my newspaper, you'd see that cutting back on the distribution of subsidized food isn't the end of the government policy. There's to be a major extension of public works as well." He nodded complacently. "That's as it should be. The poor must work for their food just like everybody else. Not the government's place to affect economic conditions. State handouts will only make the people dependent on the government. And it's perfectly sound economic theory that Irish property should pay for Irish poverty."

"Fine, then. Let it pay. Let Lanarks' Bawn pay. Reduce your rents!"

"Aye, I will. Just as soon as Lord Londonderry reduces mine."

"The Marquess of Downshire has reduced his rents by thousands of pounds. And promised his people free seed for spring planting."

"Aye, but he's not my landlord, is he? And if His Highness of Downshire chooses to pauperize himself, it doesn't follow that the rest of us need do the same. Use your common sense, lad. The rents are fixed with due regard to bad seasons as well as good. I don't hear anyone arguing that I should collect higher rents when the harvest is good. And now I have to pay iniquitously high rates on these lavish and wasteful public works."

Andrew began pacing, his fists clenched. "All right. Forget the rents. Forget the economic theory. These people are starving. I don't just mean not enough food or poor-quality food. I mean no food. Nothing to eat but boiled seaweed! How can people like this be expected to pay free market prices for imported grain?" His voice rose with every sentence.

It had been four months since Ireland had been stunned by the failure of the second potato crop. Not just a bad harvest. Not just heavy losses. Total failure. There was hardly a potato in Ireland, a land where two-thirds of the population was entirely dependent on that single item for sustenance and a healthy man was accustomed to eating ten pounds of tatties a day.

The new government in London had reversed Peel's compassionate response of the year before. However, even Russell's government realized that programs of road building would not be enough in the hardest-hit west. So, the government established corn depots along the Atlantic seaboard as far north as County Donegal. Andrew could only hope that Brendan MacHenry's family would have a share of the supplies that the paper said were to arrive next month. If the people could survive that long. And the winter storms had set in—worse storms than even the oldest residents held in their memories.

Andrew strode stiffly from the room. He and his grandfather had fought the same verbal battle every night for months. Andrew still had made no progress.

Yet he couldn't entirely blame his grandfather. Andrew himself would have had no idea how dire the situation was if he hadn't seen it with his own eyes. It was one thing to be told the crops failed and people were hungry. It was another thing to spend days riding by black, desolate fields.

To sit inside a cabin and realize that the food on his own plate, freely given by his hosts, was all they had—maybe all they would have for many days.

Jay Lanark had not seen the despair in their eyes. He did not wonder if they were surviving even now. Jay did not know what it was to smell the black rot with every breath he took. Andrew knew the stench would never leave him.

But if the government measures were inadequate, and Grandfather Lanark could not be shaken from his comfortable fireside, at least Andrew had his own strong arms. He would use them carrying what he could to the clachan. He strode downstairs to the kitchen. "Mrs. B," he addressed the comfortable housekeeper, "I want you to load every basket we have with bread and meal while I hitch up the cart."

He turned without waiting for an answer. But once beyond the shelter of the house, he'd advanced no more than ten feet toward the stable when the wind whipped blinding snow in his face. Driving to Strangford would be impossible in this.

Back in the kitchen, he found both Mrs. Berkley and her butler husband arranging supplies on the long, scrubbed table in the center of the room. "It'll have to wait until tomorrow, Mrs. B. The storm is fierce."

"Aye. As you say, sir. But if you'll permit me, this isn't the way to be going about it."

"What do you mean?" he flared. "Don't tell me you're going to lecture me on market economics, too!"

"I don't know anything about that, sir. But these Quaker people, they have the right of it, to my way of thinking."

"Oh? And what's that?" Andrew didn't mean to sound so caustic, but he had been preached at quite enough for one night.

The sturdy Mrs. Berkley, however, didn't flinch. "Soup boilers. Make soup, let the people come. Hot on the spot, no questions asked. Public works is all right. But how would Lord John Russell like to build a road on an empty stomach? That's what I'd like to know."

"Mrs. B, you're a genius!" Andrew threw his arms around her full form. "You could instruct Parliament."

From that moment Andrew was determined to do something. If Irish property was to pay for Irish poverty, then he would see to it that Lanarks' Bawn did its share, in spite of Grandfather Lanark's intransigency.

He knew that many landlords were taking vigorous action, giving what employment they could to all who applied. To be fair, even Grandfather had made some movement in that direction—until bad weather halted construction on the long gallery. Now, the second crop failure seemed to offer a propitious time to start again. As there were no potatoes to harvest, the laborers had as well be put to work gathering stones to build walls—but stones could not be pried from frozen earth.

Grandfather, following the example of Lord Londonderry, refused to join the numerous County Down landlords who had waived part of their year's rents. Ten percent off the one pound fifty per acre annual rent could mean the difference in survival to the clachan. And some landlords had gone so far as to wipe off a half year's rent and promise free seed for spring planting.

It was a hopeful prospect if the cottiers survived until spring, Andrew considered as the wind flung another blast of snow against the windows. He was stopped for the night. He felt helpless, but there had to be something he could do against the horror of hunger and despair pressing down on their land.

His mind flicked westward to the bare, black interior of a stone cottage. It had been four—almost five—months since he had left Bridget with all the food and cash he had. How long could such supplies have lasted? How long had it been since any in the MacHenry hut had gone to sleep with a full stomach? Was the frail old Brendan even still alive? Did he have strength left to play his harp?

And Dermot. There had been disturbances in places where supplies of food for distribution had been quickly depleted. Had that angry young man taken part in such brawls—and earned a broken head for it?

And Bridget. He could not think of her apart from her gleaming hair and eyes and golden laugh, knowing that such radiance would be the first sacrifice to the god of hunger. Famine ate the shine off life first. Then it gnawed in the darkness.

But Andrew would light a candle. Somehow.

· · ·

The next morning, the snow lay six inches deep on the level. What level there was. Mostly it lay in drifts reaching halfway up to the windows and leaving the roads blocked. It was two days before Andrew could take the loaves of bread, jars of preserves, and bags of meal and beans to the clachan. It remained bitterly cold, but the sun that managed to struggle though by mid-afternoon melted the snow where it had been blown thin on the roads.

There were few others out yet, and little wonder—even in his warmest, thick woolen coat, Andrew shivered. Conor O'Brien was the first person he saw. Andrew pulled his cart to a halt and greeted their stable hand.

It seemed that even the lad's freckles had faded. "I'm right sorry I haven't been up to the horses. I was after walking through the fields earlier, but Da said I'd get stuck in a drift." He squared his shoulders. "I wouldn't have, though."

"He was right, Conor." Andrew held out a hand to boost the boy onto the bench beside him. "You help me with these bags, then you can get up to your horses. They'll be right glad to see you." It was a pleasure to see the light come to the boy's eyes at the sight of food. "Go ahead and eat a bun now. It'll give you strength for carting the others."

The bap disappeared almost whole into the boy's mouth —long before they pulled up before the O'Brien door. Andrew was even happier that he had given Conor some bread when he realized what Conor had eaten for breakfast. He could smell the boiling seaweed. It was only marginally less foul than the stink of rotten tatties.

Andrew heard an infant crying inside the cottage of Elfrith and Seamus O'Brien. Since outraging Jay Lanark by marrying her papist, the girl from Edinburgh who had been nursemaid to Andrew had borne nearly a babe a year. As near as Andrew could remember, more than half of them had survived, so this cottage must house six or more hungry mouths. He knocked on the door.

It was opened by a girl of four or five.

At the end of the room Elfrith sat by the fireplace, a weeping babe on her lap. Had he not known, he would have thought this hollow-eyed woman to be the grandmother.

"I've brought some supplies to help you through the cold spell." Andrew set a basket and his largest bag of meal on the table.

"That's verra kind of you, Andrew Armstrong."

"Only fair." He smiled. "You once fed me when I needed it." He meant the remark as a kindness. He hoped the difference in station wouldn't add to her embarrassment. She had made her choice. "Where's Seamus?" Only the younger children were in evidence.

"Gone to the mill in Newtownards for the weaving."

"Aye." Andrew nodded. "That's good."

The fact that the economy of this area included linen and cotton weaving and the growing of wheat, oats, and barley would help them through this disaster if anything would. There seemed nothing more to say, so Andrew bade his former nurse good day.

. . .

He was turning the cart onto the main road when he spotted the Harrowby carriage approaching. He pulled to the side and waved. It had been long since there had been any opportunity for socializing. To his surprise, Wilma herself was driving.

Andrew caught his breath. How long had it been since he had seen her? A rim of white rabbit fur framed the hood of her dark green cape, setting off her dark ringlets and emerald eyes perfectly. He opened his mouth to greet her, but "Miss Harrowby," was all that came out.

She wasted no time on preliminaries. "Are you coming to the meeting? What a fine thing, to be sure. I'd hoped to see you there."

He had to admit he had no idea what she was talking about.

"The relief committee. There's grand plans under way, they say. We must do all we can. Selma would have come, too, but mother's not well, so she stayed with her."

"Then you must allow me to drive you." As Harrowby's Dale was closer than Lanarks' Bawn, Andrew left his cart there, and they went on together into Comber.

Andrew must have been the only person in the area who hadn't known of the meeting. He struggled to find an empty hitching post to tether the Harrowby horse to. And they were late to arrive. As they ascended the wide, dark wood interior staircase to the first floor, they could hear the ringing tones of the speaker even before they could make out his words. Andrew and Wilma slipped into seats near the back of the hall.

Wilma, who was experienced in charity work, whispered to Andrew that the portly gentleman speaking from the podium was one of the guardians of the Newtownards workhouse.

"The poor and destitute are pressing on the workhouse beyond its powers of reception. Our numbers have nearly doubled, and the walls will hold no more. The lamentable fact is that the workhouse is inadequately equipped to discharge our obligations to the poor."

He paused, giving a moment for his statements to have their effect, then took a step forward. Adam noted his long, thick sideburns and the black silk stock above his white waistcoat. He was an impressive figure. He spoke firmly, increasing his volume slightly. "Our Board of Guardians has voted—unanimously, I am pleased to say—to submit a petition to the House of Commons. We will be asking Parliament to grant us permission to distribute food to those in need without their having to be admitted to the workhouse. It is our belief that such outdoor aid can do much to relieve the distress."

Andrew nodded, and felt a spark of hope that sensible measures were being taken. Sadly, the speech that had been delivered on such a full head of steam, ended on a doubtful note. "I must report, however, that we deem it unlikely such permission will be granted."

A pinch-faced man in a black frock coat jumped to his feet just three rows ahead of Andrew. "You much relieve my mind, sir," he cried waving an arm at the speaker. "Outdoor relief, indeed. Encourage dependency and promote pauperism, that's all you'll accomplish."

Now he turned sideways to address most of the audience. "If they need aid, let them come to the workhouse. That's the system. These people have to learn to live with the system."

A scattered response of "Huzza" and "Hear, hear" met his declarations.

"Many of them would rather die." Attention shifted to a tall man in a black cassock on the other side of the room.

Andrew wasn't well enough acquainted with clerical garments to know whether the speaker was from the papacy or prelacy. But from the drawing back he sensed in the hall, it was certain the man wasn't Presbyterian.

"Then let them make their choice. It's a free country." The first speaker flipped the skirts on his coat and resumed his seat. There was scattered applause.

But the tall cleric stood firm. "The entire poor law and workhouse system is particularly alien to the native Irish. The peasantry here is tied to the land with a special feeling —as a mother for her child. Entrance to the workhouse requires giving up the lease on the final two or three acres that have sustained their family for generations. It is the loss of hope and dignity—the final damnation."

Heads nodded or shook in about equal numbers.

"Not government's business to run around the country feeding people. Let them work for it." The frock-coated man's features grew sharper yet.

Andrew was on his feet, a retort rising in his throat, when he was cut off by the chairman's ushering a small woman in a plain black dress and bonnet to the front of the room.

"You couldn't have given our special guest a better introduction, my friend." The chairman flashed a toothy grin at the pinch-faced speaker. "Mrs. Emelia Foxe has come to us from the Religious Society of Friends to speak about the very thing you suggest—voluntary soup kitchens."

It was a moment before Andrew realized how neatly the chairman had turned the man's own speech against him. He resumed his seat and joined in the welcoming applause for the lady, who managed to look pleasant in spite of the fact that she didn't smile.

"Gentlemen." Then seeing a few other women present, she added, "And ladies. I am no stranger to dealing with the problems of poverty and hunger. I come to ye from Liverpool where I have spent many years feeding the families of out-of-work dockers. And I want to assure ye all that many in yere position on the other side of the water are not insensible to the struggles ye face. Many British charities are vigorous in their dedication to collecting funds and sending contributions to committees in Ireland. But we of the Society of Friends prefer a more direct approach."

The room, that had seemed on the brink of turmoil only moments earlier, calmed as the soft, yet resonant voice commanded attention. As her hearers caught the rhythms of her strange speech they seemed to relax.

"It is our goal to establish a network of soup boilers the length and width of Ireland. People so ravished by hunger that they are scarcely able to crawl cannot break stones to build roads."

Andrew burst into applause and did not stop when narrowed eyes and raised brows turned toward him.

Emelia Foxe's voice reached to the back of the hall without strain. "For each soup kitchen we establish we will supply a boiler and money to buy ingredients to fill those pots. We have many workers, but we need more. We would invite those who would like so to do to join us."

And with that, she folded her hands before her and stood with solemn, quiet dignity, her eyes cast downward.

A jumble of questions and replies echoed around the room:

"And who's to run these kitchens?"

"Where do you mean to put them?"

"What do you propose fulling yer pots with?"

After a few moments, though, it seemed that one question reigned supreme: "And who will receive this charity broth?"

"Aye, good question. Must keep in mind there's many good Protestants going hungry as well."

"Hear, hear!"

"Take care of our own."

"It's only right."

"But most Protestants have fishing rights, at least."

"And whose fault is that if it isn't the shiftless Irish

themselves? Lived on an island for two thousand years and never developed a fishing industry—I ask you!"

"Gentlemen, gentlemen." The chairman banged on the table before him until water sloshed from his glass. "Mrs. Foxe has the floor, gentlemen."

Emelia Foxe's only indication that she was aware of the dissension in the room was an almost imperceptible raising of her chin as she raised her eyes to make contact with her hearers. "Indeed, gentlemen, yere points are well made. Let me assure ye that we have the strictest order for distribution of our relief."

Andrew strained forward. Was it possible that the ghost of a smile lurked at the corners of the solemn speaker's mouth?

Certainly, there was no mistaking her effect on her listeners as some of the more agitated speakers leaned back in their chairs. The pinch-faced man nodded and folded his arms across his chest. "Aye well, that's mighty comforting to know."

Now, for the first time, Mrs. Foxe did raise her voice. "Our soup kitchens will be open only to hungry people. All hungry people." She looked directly at her sharpest challenger, and now there was no suggestion of a smile. "With no preference on the ground of religious persuasion." She took her seat quietly amid the uproar that followed that announcement.

"Not Christian. Charity begins at home."

"We must feed our own first. Bible says so."

"It's not right to encourage those people in their heathen idolatry."

"If they're too lazy to break rocks, then that's their choice. The public works are there. Let them work. I pay my rates—blasted steep ones, too."

Despite vigorous application of his gavel, the chairman could establish no order. At last, after one more sharp rap, he shouted, "Gentlemen, be dismissed!" He stepped down from the podium.

With the meeting at an end, the hall quickly cleared of combative speakers airing their sentiments. The air continued to vibrate with contention after the door slammed shut on the last of them.

But there were others who stayed.

Throughout the proceedings, Andrew had become aware of Wilma's drawing closer to the edge of her seat. Now she sprang to her feet. "Isn't she magnificent! I knew there had to be something I could do, but I had no idea what." Her words were addressed to Andrew, but without waiting for him, she hurried up the hall to the small group surrounding the small Quaker woman.

"We will open kitchens in Comber and Newtownards next month. We should be happy, indeed, of hands to help prepare and serve the soup. We would also be grateful for additional contributions of food or money."

A variety of questions rose.

"A most sustaining soup," the speaker replied to the inquiry as to what the famine pots would contain. "Perhaps thee would care to see." She pulled a handful of papers from the black bag she carried and handed them around.

Andrew read the recipe over Wilma's shoulder:

1 oxhead

28 pounds turnips

3 1/2 pounds onions

7 pounds carrots

21 pounds pea meal

14 pounds Indian cornmeal

28 gallons water

Nutritious, indeed. A boiler of such a soup distributed daily would do much to relieve distress. He would enjoy working beside Wilma in the effort. And yet, as he thought of the rancor that still hung in the corners of the room, it seemed that even those with full bellies suffered from their own form of desperation. It was hard to define what bothered him. It seemed frivolous to worry about matters of philosophy in the face of the suffering that pressed down on their land. And yet he had seen in his own grandfather, as in some of the speakers tonight, a joylessness that no soup boiler, however nutritious the ingredients filling it, could feed.

There had to be a better answer to the problem of human suffering than a potato.

CHAPTER FIVE

Just one potato. If only she had just one. Bridget hugged her brychan closer to her and edged toward the banked turfs. She'd been dreaming she walked in the field, feeling the soft brown earth under her feet, smelling the clean, fresh air as the sun shone on row after row of healthy green leaves. And then she had gone in and boiled a great black pot of tatties to set before Dermot and *Seanathair* with the sweet butter she had churned that morning and a cool jug of fresh buttermilk.

Sure, and it had been sweet, but the memory made the clawing of her stomach all the worse. She listened to the howling wind whip snow against the side of the cottage. Would the weather be too bad for Dermot to work tomorrow? All labor on the roads had ceased when snow gripped the land in as tight a hand as the blight had last summer. And so, the last drops of life were being squeezed out of Ireland between the strangleholds of famine and frost.

While summer lasted, there had been much she could do to fill the MacHenry cook pot. Nettles and dandelions were never so nasty as seaweed. Berries grew in the bog. And she had become clever at trapping birds in the hedgerow. She had learned to weave a clever net from strands of fibrous grasses, then spread it on bushes with a few bright berries peeking through. Many a small warbler had entangled a tiny talon in the mesh she never strayed far from.

But that all seemed as long ago as the days of digging tatties from their bed. Now there were only rocks to crush. And today there would not even be that, as there had not been yesterday or the day before. And anyway, one could not make soup from rocks.

She reached beyond the edge of her pallet to where Madoo slept beside Brendan. Her fingers closed in his long, gray hair, only a slightly darker shade than *Seanathair's*. How many winters had they spent huddled beside the fire, keeping each other warm, man and dog? As long as Bridget could remember—since the days when Madoo was a squirming pup begging to have his pink stomach scratched. And then Brendan had been able to see to do it. The memory brought tears to Bridget's eyes. All so long ago. How could it be so long? And everything so changed?

She knew she was putting off the inevitable moment. Now she understood how *Seanathair* could go so far away in his mind for such long times. And she was glad he had that escape. But that could not be her way. She was the woman. She must have something in the cook pot if Dermot was to have strength to crush rocks and if *Seanathair* was to live through the winter. She crossed herself with a plea that the solution offered for today wouldn't be a blow that would kill him.

"Come on, boy. It's time." Her brychan still wrapped around her shoulders, she took the knife used for cutting seed potatoes in happier times. The wind wrenched the door out of her hand, but she managed to close it before kneeling with her arms around Madoo. She would have liked to go farther away from the hut, but she dare not in the snow.

She knew where to make the slit. The animal was too weak even to cry out. He settled his head on her lap as the warm blood ran into the snow. It was as if he knew he was giving himself for *Seanathair*. It was the last thing he could do for his lifelong companion.

Even as scrawny as the creature was, they would be fed for a week, perhaps two. First the roast. Then the bones and entrails boiled for broth. If *Seanathair* would eat. She did not know what she would say to him.

He woke when the smell of roasting meat filled the cabin. Far stronger than the usual scent of burning peat. Bridget watched his sticklike fingers search the pallet and earthen floor beyond for a clutch of stiff, brindled hair. Then the thin old nostrils quivered. His whole body stiffened to a sitting position, the hands still searching in empty air, the nose smelling.

Bridget left her spit-turning to fling herself into her

grandfather's arms. "*Seanathair*. It's so sorry I am, *Seanathair*. So sorry."

He patted her back. "I know, *Cailin*. I know, girl." He said no more about it. But when she put a meaty bone in his hands, silver tears trailed from his blind eyes.

Later, he took up his harp. It had been long silent. The second crop failure had taken all music from the land. But a *seanchaidh* must hold wake for his loved ones. And hearing his songs, for the first time in months Bridget thought of the debt she owed to Andrew Armstrong. She had done nothing about the learning of Brendan MacHenry's songs. The hunger had driven all thought of anything but survival from every mind.

But now she thought of the kind stranger from a different world who claimed some sort of relationship to their family. The whole matter had sounded like a tale of the fairies. Perhaps Andrew Armstrong himself had been but a fairy's conjuring. But no fairy would leave coins. And it was that brass and silver that had made all the difference. Andrew Armstrong's coins were to thank for the MacHenrys still having thatch over their heads.

Even in front of the fire, Bridget shuddered, thinking of their many neighbors who had been evicted when they had no means of paying their rents. Turned out on the roads with the snows coming. Staring into the glowing peats, she could see it all again. Weeks before the constabulary came with their signed notices from Lord Grangeton, one could feel the fear. The smell of the terror was as sharp and rancid as that from the bins of rotted potatoes. Families huddled inside their thatched cabins, wondering if they would be next. For none of the croppies in their clachan or anywhere the length of the Atlantic coast had been able to pay their rent. Some landlords were lenient. Lord Grangeton was not.

And so, inexorably, the constabulary would come. To two or three huts a week, sometimes to as many as one a day until an entire area was cleared out.

"Aye, and that pinchfist of an overseer Grady Erskine enjoys every one of them." Dermot, his mouth still warm with a swig of last year's poteen—for there had been no potato peelings to make whiskey in the hidden stills this year—would curse Lord Grangeton's manager. "Can't wait to get us all cleared out, he can't. Wants the land for grazing. You think he has the constabulary smash the cabins just so no one can live in them again? Nae. Doing his filthy work for him, they are. Nice, smooth pastureland as far as the eye can see, fattening cattle for the English market to feed fat Englishmen and fatten his purse—that's Grangeton's goal."

Whatever the landlord's goal, or his overseer's, it came to the same thing: the constabulary in a circle around the door, banging hard enough to break it down if they didn't open. The smell of fear coming out before the ragged family emerged from their black hole, clutching each other and what few rags they could hold around themselves. Some tried screams, some prayers, some physical resistance.

The reply was always the same and always swift. Families whose people had lived on that land, in that cottage, for time out of mind were no more than a few yards down the road before battering rams had scattered the stones that had provided the only shelter they had ever known. The last glimpse any of them had of their home was black smoke curling from the thatch of the fallen roof.

The lucky ones were done first, before the workhouse was full. Officials did what they could. They threw up shacks in the workhouse yards to provide some shelter, but the buildings in every county were so filled there was barely sitting space on the floor. Only death made room for newcomers.

Bridget forced her mind back to *Seanathair's* song. She must keep the songs in her memory. If Andrew Armstrong should ever return for his payment, she must have it for him. All her grandfather's songs of saints and fairies, of beauty and hardship, of people, animals, and plants, she must remember them.

For Andrew, yes, but more for *Seanathair*. His songs were himself. To preserve his songs would be to preserve the man. Bridget knew that someday, a day not far distant, in spite of her best efforts, the songs would be all that she would have left of this beloved man.

She would sit on the pallet next to him just as Madoo had always done. "Teach me the songs, *Seanathair*." Then sometimes hunger rose like a black fog in her brain, and she hadn't strength even to hear the words. But after a time, when the weakness passed, she would turn to her grandfather, who had let the harp droop to his tattered brychan. "I'll fetch a cup of kelp broth, *Seanathair*. Strength it will give you for another song."

And sometimes she must needs crawl to the pot because there was not support in her legs to hold her. Yet even so weak in body and in spirit, Bridget carried on until fear closed in again. Was there anything to carry on for? Was the land itself dead? Had the very dirt died like the countless bodies it covered?

Where would it end? When they were all dead—every last person in Ireland a corpse? And who would bury the last one? Would God send a rain to wash the land clean then? Or would it ever be thus, world without end?

One morning she woke to hear a bird singing in the hedgerow. It was a faint, hungry-sounding warble, but it penetrated the stone walls of the cottage and reached Bridget's heart like a glimmer of hope. Just two weeks ago there had been a heavy snowfall. Yet this faint trill said that, somehow, they had survived another winter. Perhaps the land would be green and fertile again as it had once been.

But then a sound far louder and more penetrating than the bird's entered the hut. It was the far too familiar wail that struck her with terror every time she heard it. She went to the door to watch the pitiful sight pass across the frozen earth.

Eight or nine keening people—rag-covered sticks—followed a man, aged in appearance if not in years, whose stooped shoulders told more than the bundles he carried of the desperation that pushed him to his destiny. But it wasn't fear for the departing stranger that gripped Bridget. It was fear for her brother.

The road to the bay ran past their door, and Bridget never failed to notice the quiet way Dermot looked at the emigrants trudging down the path, belongings tied in pitiful bundles, their relatives following along, wailing as if seeing them to their graves.

And, indeed, the partings were well named "American wakes," for those who set out to cross the water in the over-crowded, creaking ships to America or Canada or New Zealand were as lost to their families as if they were dead. Even if they survived the voyage, they would not be returning to Ireland. Ever.

Bridget clutched at her heart as if she could grasp the fear and fling it from her. Dermot and *Seanathair* were the only family she had ever known. She knew she must lose the frail old man someday. But Dermot, the big brother she had trailed after since she took her first steps—what would she do without him? Her first fears upon waking every morning—even before she feared there would be nothing at all for the pot that day—was that she would find *Seanathair* dead on his pallet or that this would be the day Dermot would tell her he had booked passage.

Winter storms had slowed the emigrations, even as they increased the hunger, for the ships could not sail. So, people lay in their huts and breathed their last, rather than dying on one of the coffin ships.

But a bird had sung this morning.

Bridget turned from the sorrowful group disappearing down the road and gathered the strength to look her brother full in the eye. No matter what she saw there, she must face it. "It will be better now, Dermot. Even today, perhaps, the works will be starting again."

"Aye." His tone was always bitter now. But perhaps it relieved the pain inside. "Oh, aye. Those with strength to lift a hammer will do so. Building roads that go nowhere and lining them with famine walls—as if one could wall out the famine!" He spat.

"We can buy seed, Dermot. We must have seed."

This year it would be a pitiful handful, if tubers for planting were available at all. But they must be, or there would be nothing to go on with. Planting seed so there could be a harvest was the very essence of hope. It was seed that made life go on.

Planting time had always been her favorite. Memories she thought lost came back to her. Springtime when she was a child. She almost thought she could remember her mother, a fair woman with a babe in one arm, another wane tugging at her apron, and her belly rounding under her skirt...

She returned to thoughts of planting. Always she and Dermot had worked together, pushing their feet in rhythm on the blades of their loys, turning the first long, thin spade of sod on St. Patrick's Day to make beds for the potatoes. A new crop, no matter how sparse, meant new hope. No matter how deep the hunger, how far off the harvest, seed in the field meant life.

Planting had always been a communal thing. All the croppies from the helter-skelter cluster of stone cottages that dotted Lord Grangeton's estate gathered to hear Father Lynch begin the labor by blessing the fields. As soon as he was gone, Daddo O'Casey, the only man in the clachan older than Brendan MacHenry, would spit into the wind and toss a handful of straw into the air to keep the storms at bay, while his daughter Mairead crumbled a sweet cake to appease the fairies. And then they would all turn to their digging.

But this year, even if they could obtain seed, it would be different. The O'Caseys had been among the first to be evicted. Only four or five of the huts on the estate remained with their walls unbroken and their thatch intact. Grady Erskine was a thorough man.

A few weeks later, on the day Dermot came in with a handful of seed potatoes, Bridget and her brother put their backs to turning the beds. It was a lonely process, for fear is an icy companion. And the apparition of the coming months was always before them. Even in the best of years, the blue months were there to be gotten through. And now the phantom of what if hung over everything. What if they couldn't hang on until harvest? What if they hung on but couldn't pay the rent? What if… no, the specter of another crop failure was too bleak to imagine.

On Good Friday Bridget planted the few ridges of potatoes that her seeds would fill. And Dermot returned to his futile, endless road building.

"Dermot!" Bridget could not give words to the fear that gripped her at her first look at him only two hours later.

Sure, and he was returning too early in the day, for didn't the works crews stay at their shovels and sledgehammers until dark? But it was more the manner of his return than the hour of it. She had not seen such anger in him since the day he had heard of Lord Russell's policy that Ireland would export the only food that could feed its people. What could have happened to make him react in such anger now? She feared to ask.

"Dermot? What is it?"

"The public works are to stop."

"When?"

"Now. Whole system to be done up by summer. Government decided men should stay home and work their fields to produce this year's harvest."

"But that's months away!"

She started to signal him to speak more softly—she didn't want to worry *Seanathair*. But it was no use. The old man sat on a bench against the sunny wall of the house. His eyes were blind, but his ears were keen. *Seanathair* knew.

"What will we do?" she barely had strength to ask.

"The government will provide soup. We are to be given tickets."

Even if the stirabout of boiled Indian corn would keep

them alive, soup tickets would not pay the rent. Only the few precious barley seeds Bridget had planted around the edge of the field could do that. If the heads made well. If the rain and sun came at the right time. If the potatoes were good so they could sell the barley. If—if—if. Survival was always a thin line. But never before had their whole existence hung by such a spider's thread.

A curl of black smoke caught her attention. "Faith, is it the O'Malleys? Have they been evicted now? How can that be? They planted their potatoes not two weeks ago."

Dermot shook his head. "It's not the constabulary this time."

"Then—"

"It's the fever."

"The whole family? Cathal? Finola? The wanes?" Last week Finola had taken to her pallet with the bloody flux— one of the common signs of famine fever. But the whole family? Bridget slumped to the ground. Who would be next? Would the fever take them all like that? Had they survived two winters of famine and escaped eviction only to be carried off by the dropsy. A soft tune reached her ears, more as if the harp strings were moved by the wind than by Brendan MacHenry's fingers.

No. Bridget squared her shoulders. *No.* She would not give in. As long as there was breath in her, they would survive. She and her family and the songs they had made for hundreds of years—they would survive, and Ireland would be the better for it.

CHAPTER SIX

That spring of 1847 Andrew was quite certain he had found the answer to many of his longings. Indeed, as satisfying as he had found working with the Quaker Society to be throughout the dark, cold winter months, he realized that the light and warmth he felt was from quite another source than the ever-simmering soup boilers. Although the work itself, and the good they were able to achieve, certainly offered a sense of fulfillment as well.

Amelia Foxe and her team of hard-working Quakers had done all they promised and more, installing huge boilers in a renovated warehouse to cook the soup for which they provided most of the ingredients to be prepared by the army of volunteers they organized. The *Belfast News Letter* reported that across Ireland some three million people were fed each day in kitchens just like this one.

And it was said that Mrs. Foxe's meat-based soup recipe

provided a far healthier meal than the stirabout of Indian corn provided by the government, as many people fed only that were falling victim to famine fever, bloody flux, or famine dropsy. Such scourges were proving a danger even to the better-fed who worked among the famine victims. There were reported cases of doctors and philanthropy workers succumbing alongside the sick and starving they ministered to.

Andrew shook his head. Now was not the time for such contemplations. There was work to focus on. He seized a bucket, filled it from the nearest of the three bubbling cauldrons, and carried it to the row of tables lined with women standing behind enormous serving pots. All Andrew's earlier thoughts fled as Wilma moved aside from her pot to allow him to fill it with the steaming soup.

Her soft brown hair curled around her face and her cheeks flushed pink from the heat of the liquid as she swirled the contents of her pot with a long-handled ladle, then dropped it and wiped her hands on the long white apron that swathed her full skirt and hugged her tiny waist. Wilma surveyed the line of servers all standing at the ready and dipped her head in a satisfied nod. "There now, Andrew." She paused to offer a smile that gave him hope the answer to her happiness might lay in the same direction as his. "You can open the doors. The soup is ready."

He moved toward the heavy wooden doors creaking with the weight of hunger pressing against them. "And the loaves?" he asked over his shoulder.

"Aye, the last batch done."

The ovens were manned all night by Quakers come from England to bake the bread they distributed with the soup.

Andrew and two other regular volunteers lifted the bar, the doors groaned open, and the waiting line of starving people shuffled forward. That was perhaps the most disheartening aspect of this work—watching how the line grew longer every week—and moved more slowly. When they began last November, the hungry horde had pushed and hammered against the doors until Andrew sometimes feared a brawl. But now, they didn't have the spirit to fight or complain. The gray line of ghosts crept onward, each shadowy specter holding out a battered tin cup or cracked bowl.

From behind their long row of tables the serving women filled each extended vessel with the thick mixture of vegetables in meat broth. Andrew held a basket of warm, crusty brown loaves. He put one into each birdlike claw held out to him. The line wavered as fog blowing over the bog. The wraiths shifted, and Andrew held out another bun.

So on for hours. It would continue until they came to the end of the line or the bottom of the boilers. When the wooden ladles scraped on the black iron and not another bit of carrot or parsnip could be scratched off, and the last supplicant left the long rows of wooden benches that lined the tables filling the hall, Mrs. Foxe's Society of Friends took charge. A team of Quakers began washing the vessels and refilling them with the prescribed meat, vegetables, meal, and water, while Andrew, Wilma, and other volunteers turned to sweeping the rough stone floor and wiping the tables and benches so recently filled with the skeletal imprints of what had once been vigorous, laughing, brawling, human beings. The cycle never ended, for tomorrow the need would all be there again, except with a degree more of desperation, as each day the hunger bore deeper.

Today as every day—for Wilma insisted on working without a break, and he would not let her face the task alone—Andrew soon shifted his thoughts from the dismal scene before him to the happier time he anticipated. Flashes of guilt caught him out for contemplating his own joy in the face of so much suffering. And yet how could it be otherwise with Wilma beside him? Soon he must speak to her. He was almost certain of her answer. How could she not return his favor when he felt so much for her? She must feel something for him beyond gratitude for his help and companionship.

He would speak to her tonight when they were driving back to Harrowby's Dale with the shared satisfaction of having helped so many people survive yet another day. Knowing that together they had kept absolute starvation at bay for another few hours, they could relax from their labors while others prepared for the next day's battle.

Or should he speak to her father first? Again, he did not despair of success, for Mr. Harrowby had ever made him welcome at Harrowby's Dale. Andrew had known a worrying time last winter when Mrs. Harrowby was too sick to leave her bed. Would Wilma have to put her own happiness aside to care for her mother and keep house for her father? For Selma, who had taken on that task so naturally when first Mrs. Harrowby fell ill, was now looking forward to her own wedding. Thomas Price had not been so slow in the asking as Andrew Armstrong had been.

All through January, Andrew had worried. But when the last of February's snowstorms melted, Mrs. Harrowby had left her bed. Everyone's spirits rose. And Selma had ordered a length of white silk from London. Thomas' successful suit no longer appeared as a barrier to Andrew but rather a good omen.

Yes. He would speak. Tonight.

"Oh!" A sharp cry from Wilma jerked him from his daydream. "That poor woman!"

Andrew handed his ladle to one of the kitchen workers and hurried around the serving bar.

He had seen it before—indeed, the incidents seemed to be coming more frequently of late—but he could never accustom himself to the idea of people's being so starved that getting food into their stomachs made them faint. The woman's three children were crying and pulling at her, terrified.

He moved the children aside and put a piece of bun in each pair of grimy hands. "Here now, your mother will be all right. Let her rest." He turned to the oldest girl. "When she wakens, see that she takes only small bites. Why haven't you come before?"

The baffled looks that met this speech told him his effort at communication had been wasted. The family spoke only Irish. He expressed his instructions by pantomime, then resumed his serving.

"Will she be all right?" Wilma asked.

How could he answer that? Would any of them be all right? What was the use of recovering today only to starve tomorrow? He shrugged and tipped a scoop of meal into the bowl held out to him. "They seem to be wandering poor. Most likely come down from the mountains. Her husband probably died."

"Then they don't have any place to stay."

Wilma spoke matter-of-factly. They were all past any level of shock at a new horror. Whenever it seemed things couldn't get worse, they got worse. And all the time Andrew kept in the back of his mind the fact that eastern Ulster was the least hard hit of any of Ireland. Bad as things were here, they were worse elsewhere. And as the destitute drifted in from other areas, the situation worsened here.

As always, such a thought made him wonder about Bridget. Western Connacht was the most devastated area in Ireland. Had she managed to survive? He had not forgotten that he told her he would return. But that was not possible. Not now. Everything had stopped when the hunger descended upon the land.

"What will they do?" Wilma repeated, bringing Andrew's focus back to the little huddle of bones and rags on the floor.

"Workhouse."

"Andrew, no!"

The ultimate horror. The end of all hope. But what else

was there? Looking at the scene before him, Andrew could think of nothing else. The outside aid provided by voluntary soup kitchens was sufficient—just—for those with their own cabins. Only the workhouse provided sleeping shelter as well as food. "They won't object. They have no property to surrender."

Wilma nodded. "We can take them when we're through here."

Andrew groaned. That would take at least an hour more. Maybe two. The woman and three squalling children in the carriage. And then, after facing the dismaying facts of the workhouse, he and Wilma would both be drained emotionally and physically. He could not speak of their future happiness tonight.

"Andrew? They canna walk there."

The woman had wakened from her faint. The oldest child was spooning bits of meal into her mother's mouth. Apparently, Andrew's pantomime had been successful. But the woman only half sat up, and her scrawny throat looked too frail even to swallow the stirabout.

He sighed. "No. They cannot walk."

Andrew had regularly heard reports of the appalling workhouse conditions. People held out too long before resorting to charity. They were so seriously undernourished by the time they entered that the workhouse was nothing more than a place to go to die. As he stopped the carriage before the iron fence surrounding the gray stone building, he recalled vividly the most recent report: "The great majority of new admissions are moribund when brought to us."

The somber guardian reporting had been replying to a charge that the death rate in the workhouse was unacceptably high.

"The country is rampant with disease. Many have been known to die on the road, others even as they are lifted from their beds to the cart to be brought in. Many are sent for admission merely that coffins may be provided for them at government expense."

As a matter of fact, the Board of Guardians had received complaints from the parish authorities that the graveyard was filling up with pauper dead from the workhouse. A separate burial ground for paupers was necessary. And still the workhouse bulged with 750 unwashed bodies while an additional 100 inhabited the fever hospital attached to it. A house of horrors, indeed. And yet, there was nowhere else for the destitute to go.

The woman, huddled in the back of the carriage, looked at him with famine-hollowed eyes. She descended listlessly when he indicated. The children clung to their mother silently. The youngest, barely two, never took her thumb from her mouth. Their skin was blotched and cracked from scurvy. The little boy scratched constantly at the lice living on his scalp.

The gray-uniformed matron at a table inside the door announced, "We've no place to put them." She paused. "But from the looks of things, they won't be here long." She thrust a form at Andrew.

He glanced at the information requested. "I don't know. I have no idea what their names are or where they came from."

The exhausted woman shrugged. "Then put down your name. We have to have some identity. They can sleep in the attic tonight. If they're alive tomorrow, we'll worry about it then. Probably the usual story—husband wouldn't leave his land, so he died on it. Then his family comes to the workhouse." She shook her head. "Always comes to it in the end."

It was as well that Andrew had already decided he wouldn't speak of his heart to Wilma tonight. He was too drained to talk at all. And, to all appearances, so was she. Yet her presence was a comfort. He felt her warmth, her small person. Beside him. Where he wanted her always.

Perhaps it was the fatigue that made him wonder, *Will that be enough?* Would having Wilma to wife fill all his heart's desires? He had certainly been right in his conclusion that food and pleasant surroundings were not the key, for in the midst of all the suffering they dealt with daily, he had found unspeakable happiness in her company.

So, surely, having that companionship sealed for life would be the answer. He would have the deep, settled joy inside himself that would preclude his turning into the sour, rigid man his grandfather was. Wilma's love could keep him from that if anything could. With Wilma he could defeat the Lanark curse.

A freezing rain started to fall before they reached Harrowby's Dale. He pulled the carriage as close as he could to the door and hurried Wilma inside, holding his coat over her bonnet and mantle. At the door he urged her to take care of herself. "Have a hot drink and a meal and stay warm and dry. Sleep well, Wilma. This work is too hard for you. You must rest."

Her hand rested briefly on his arm; her eyes still smiled after the exhausting day. "Dear Andrew. Don't fuss. I'm fine. It gives me such pleasure to help these poor creatures. I only wish I could do more. I draw strength from the work."

Andrew opened his mouth to argue, then realized the futility of anything he could say against such radiant confidence as Wilma's. If only he could share her certainty.

CHAPTER SEVEN

There was little that could have lifted his spirits when he entered the bawn that night, but the sight of Thomas Price sitting before the fire where he had expected to encounter only his scowling grandfather made the fatigue roll from Andrew's shoulders.

"Tammis! What a welcome sight!" He clasped his cousin's hand, then flung himself into a chair and propped his wet boots on the hob.

Berkley appeared as if by magic with a dry coat and a tray of cold meats and cheeses.

"Thank you, Berkley. Just what I need. Ah—and a bowl of spiced punch." He drank deeply. "Perhaps I'll live to fight another day." He leaned back in his chair.

Jay Lanark scowled at his grandson. "Don't know what you think you're doing, serving soup like a kitchen maid. Not so sure I hold with this whole volunteerism thing, anyway. The *Northern Whig* says indigents are pouring into

Belfast—attracted by the reputation of local charities. Bad enough having to take care of our own. We'll be overrun. And they bring disease. Importing contagion and demoralization we are."

Andrew was too exhausted to mount a reply. And in spite of the brutal attitude, there was just enough truth to what his grandfather said to give him concern.

"We pay crippling rates to keep the workhouse open," Jay Lanark continued. "That ought to be enough. Only collected seventy-five percent of my rents this year. And Price here telling me he waived half of his—besides feeding his croppies." He shook his head. "We'll all be bankrupt soon. Then who'll pay to keep the workhouse open? That's what I want to know. Be standing in your soup line myself, that's what. Alongside Lord Londonderry, no doubt. If the gentry can't pay their rents, the whole system'll crumble. You'll understand one day, boy. You'll see it my way."

"Never!" Andrew spat out the word like a poisoned dart.

His grandfather laughed. "You say that, but you'll see. It's your destiny. You're a Lanark. You're preordained. You can't escape it."

Andrew had heard the same speech every night for two years. He turned to his cousin. "Tammis, I hear I am to wish you joy. A length of ivory satin is on its way from London, even. When's the happy day to be?"

Thomas heaved a sigh, seemingly to clear the air of acrimony before turning to his own situation. "Late summer we're talking about. Aye, and it can't come too soon for me." A small smile curved his generous mouth. "But I don't know. Can't help wondering if we should put it off for a more auspicious time."

Andrew stopped with a slice of roast mutton halfway to his mouth. "Put it off? Man, if I were in your position, I'd be counting the days—if not the hours."

Thomas ran a hand through his thick black curls. "Aye, I am that."

"Then, why—" Andrew had seldom seen his light-hearted cousin so doleful.

Thomas looked into the fire. "I don't know. It's just that it seems callous when so many are dying."

"What's their dying to do with it? Can you save them by staying single? Will your marriage make their pain worse? On the contrary, when there's so little happiness in the world, it's our responsibility to do what we can to bring in a little joy. Anything to cut through this gray mist of sorrow hanging over the land."

"Gray mist of sorrow—cousin, you're a poet." Thomas paused. "Maybe there is something in what you say. And yet—this matter of the Swatara, now—it seems things just get worse and worse."

"What matter? What's the Swatara?'

Grandfather had been sitting silently, smoking his pipe. Now he burst back into the conversation. "Ha! Well you might ask, lad." He scooped the newspaper from the hearth rug beside him. "Here now, read this and learn a thing or two. You'll see what I was telling you. Disease and desolation—as if we didn't have enough of our own, now we're importing it by the shipload. Right into Belfast harbor."

Andrew took the paper and shifted his position so that the firelight fell more directly on it. Disease was the topic of the day, even above the famine itself. Widespread hunger was pressing down on much of Europe—although not with the desperation of Ireland, because only Ireland had relied on a single crop for almost all of its food supply. But particularly alarming news was the highly contagious nature of the plague-breath. The peasantry's emaciated condition left them highly susceptible to the ravages of disease, but gentry and merchants were falling victim to the pestilence as well. In Cavan alone, seven doctors had died.

Ah, there was the item Tammis had referred to. The Swatara, a vessel chock-full of emigrants to America, had for the second time been buffeted by contrary winds and forced back into Belfast harbor. Only after some of those aboard had been allowed ashore had it been discovered that typhus fever had been festering in the cramped below-deck quarters. The article quoted a campaigner for public health, Dr. Andrew Malcolm: "I have the gravest concerns that the fever may sweep from the port throughout the town. The results of such an epidemic at this time could be unthinkable."

Andrew let the paper slip from his hand. How was it possible for things to get worse? The stench and noise of the overcrowded workhouse rose in his nose and ears—and then he saw Wilma, holding a crying infant while a little boy stood beside her and scratched at lice. Body lice carried typhus.

Wilma must be warned. She took enough risk just working at the soup kitchen. It seemed everyone took risks simply living in Ireland. She must not, however, expose herself further by going to the workhouse again. He would speak to her first thing.

The next day she met him smiling, her rosy brightness chasing away his midnight alarms. He had barely handed her into the carriage when she turned to him.

"Selma and Mother are to go to the dressmaker today. We spent half the night with Selma looking at the *Journal des Demoiselles* and looping swaths of silk over her in different manners." She clapped her hands. "Oh, you must think us terribly frivolous to be thinking of such things when people are starving, but it was so lovely to spend a few hours just laughing and daydreaming as we did so often—before." She sighed. "Can it really have been only two years ago?"

Andrew smiled at the pleasant sight of a young woman thinking of dresses and future happiness. All life had stopped when the famine struck. Even those with food in their bellies had put normal activities aside to fight the hunger choking life out of their land. But his friends had found a gleam of light in the dark. And he was glad.

"You are the least frivolous woman I know. I would as soon apply the term to Emelia Foxe. And I am delighted you spent a pleasant time with your sister. If we sink with the famine victims, who will be left to minister to them?" He could see his answer much mollified her concern.

She gave him the smile that revealed her dimples. "And what do you think? Should my gown be of lavender or yellow?"

Andrew had never been consulted on a matter of fashion before. A few flowers surviving beside the lane caught his eye. "Yellow is very pretty."

She laughed but did not seem displeased.

He had not forgotten his determination to warn her to stay away from the fever-ridden workhouse, but he could not bring himself to introduce such a dismal topic. He did not want those dimples to disappear.

Besides, there would be time. After all, he was driving. He simply would not take her into an infected area. The soup kitchen was carefully scrubbed with lye soap every night by the meticulous Quakers, and he could guard her from actual contact with those she served. Perhaps they should even start washing their hands after working with the famine victims. Some advanced thinkers such as Dr. Malcolm were beginning to advise that. But in the meantime, he could enjoy Wilma's smiles.

A few days later Andrew went down to breakfast to find his grandfather brandishing the *Belfast News Letter*. "Ha, and what did I tell ye?"

"Indeed, Grandfather, quite a few things. But I'm sure

you'll inform me as to which particular one you are gloating over this morning."

"Epidemic in Belfast. Knew it was just a matter of time. From that ship, no doubt. Town full of emigrants and starving hordes from the countryside. What do they expect?"

Grandfather continued on about how the newly established Board of Health had ordered sheds put up beside the Frederick Street Hospital and a temporary hospital erected near the workhouse—and how Dr. Malcolm warned of worse to come.

But Andrew wasn't listening. How could he have let the matter lapse so long? He had to get to Wilma. He had to warn her. He hurried to the stable.

No, warning wasn't enough, he decided as he urged his horses along the lane. Wilma must give up the soup kitchen work, at least until the epidemic was past. There would be something else she could do for the poor. Sew for them. Raise chickens and give them eggs. But she must be kept safe. Why, oh why, had he waited to broach the subject? He would see that she stayed safely home today.

The Harrowby front door opened at his first knock. "Oh. Selma." He had been so prepared to launch into his lecture to Wilma that he was tongue-tied at the sight of her sister. He struggled to regain his manners. "How is our radiant bride today?"

"Just step in and have a look!" Selma dimpled almost as prettily as her twin. Tammis Price was a lucky man. She held out the sketch of a dress. Rows of lace ruffles surrounded the wide shoulder line, and the full skirt was lace from fingertips to the floor.

"Um… very pretty."

"Yes, isn't it!" Selma hugged the picture. "It was Queen Victoria's wedding dress. I'm thinking I'll have it copied."

"Yes. Very pretty. But—forgive my abruptness—but I must see your sister."

"Oh, yes, she left you a message."

"What do you mean? She knew I'd be calling for her."

"That's why she left the message. She said to tell you she'd meet you later at the kitchen."

"But I don't understand. Where is she?"

"She went with that Quaker woman—Mrs. Foxe."

"Yes, yes—"

"To buy supplies for the boilers. The kitchens are so inundated, they are starting double shifts."

"But where did they go?"

"To market, of course. Newtownards, I think. Or Belfast, maybe. A grain ship was coming into port—"

"Why didn't you stop her?" He turned on Selma with such vehemence that she dropped her fashion sketch. "Why didn't someone—"

"Did you ever try to stop Wilma when she'd her mind made up? Mother isn't well, and father's in the fields. I—"

He waited to hear no more. But halfway down the walk he turned back. "When did she leave? How long ago?"

Selma frowned, considering. "Half an hour. Maybe more."

He jumped into the carriage and sprang his horses.

There was a chance he could catch up with them on the road. Belfast. Had the girl no sense? Going to a crowded market in a town raging with typhus. Why, oh why, had he let things go so long? If anything happened, it would be all his fault.

The road to Belfast was a nightmare. And, as in a nightmare, Andrew felt a desperate urgency to hurry, yet could barely move. The road was choked with traffic going both directions—those going to the city seeking food, shelter, and medical aid, and those coming toward him, fleeing the pestilence, no doubt. A few carriages trotted smartly along, whenever possible passing lumbering farm carts. But most of the traffic was on foot, clumps of ragged humanity, clinging together for the strength to move forward. A few pushed hand barrows. Most carried pitifully small, tattered bundles—all their earthly possessions. Victims of eviction with no place to go.

Andrew's heart leaped as he passed a clattering wagon. There—just ahead—was a small black buggy of the style favored by Quakers. The two-wheeled carriage was pulled by only one horse, so Andrew's fine pair could easily overtake it if he could just get around this group shuffling in front of him. And the old man pushing a handcart. And… He flicked the reins and urged his horses forward.

"Hello!" He drew up beside the carriage and leaned around its tall, straight side. "Thank goodness I caught you—" He broke off when two bearded men in plain collars and flat, wide-brimmed hats stared at him from inside. Without another word, Andrew sped past the buggy, in spite of the narrowness of the road.

At last, he clattered over Long Bridge spanning the River Lagan and made for High Street. How would he ever find anyone in this milling mob? A ship just in, Selma had said. He turned toward Chichester Quay. Indeed, the harbor was full of tall-masted vessels, some with sails furled. How many of their holds were stuffed to the deck with fleeing human beings? Rumor said it wasn't unusual for a third of the human cargo to die en route to their new homes. Still, the billowing sails offered hope to those able to scrape together money for passage. And some landlords, no longer able to support tenants who were unable to pay their rents, paid the passage for their people.

Something was wrong here. It took Andrew several minutes to figure it out. It was the lack of sound. An uncanny quiet. In the heart of this busy port, choked with people, there was a strange silence. Hunger-weakened people moved as in a stupor. They had no energy for conversation. The predominant tone was an eerie mumble, sounding more like moaning wind than human voice.

Determined to search the market on foot, Andrew found a vacant hitching post for his team. Bags that could well contain corn were being unloaded at quayside. A great crowd was gathered around. Was Wilma in the center of those people? Breathing their plague-breath?

Looking intently at every face that happened to be framed by a round bonnet tied with black ribbons, Andrew paid little attention to the placement of his feet until he tripped over a scrawny figure and almost fell. He started to offer assistance to the fallen man, then reeled back. The man was dead. Andrew looked around for someone to help.

An old man sitting on a stump nearby shook his gray head. "Don't bother yourself. He's been there all morning. Dead cart'll be along by evening." The man gave a gap-toothed imitation of a chuckle. "Be more to keep him company by then."

Andrew backed away. Where was Wilma? Her name rose in his throat. It was all he could do to keep from shouting it.

Then a sound rose just ahead from around the sacks of grain being stacked on the quay. It was just an angry rumble, like threatening thunder, but in the atmosphere of enervation and futility it rang loud.

"Corn. From America!"

A rock struck the shoulder of a dockworker guarding the precious hoard.

"Aye. To keep my family alive!" A man lunged forward with a stick.

They were futile gestures. The dockworkers would not yield their grain. But it was enough to start a riot. Hunger-crazed men would not be denied the possibility of a few more days of life. The dock erupted in a swell of flailing clubs and hammering fists.

Andrew started to retreat. Then he saw two female figures. He pressed forward. "Wil—" A heavy stick caught him on the side of the head. His knees buckled. His last sight was of dirty, roughshod feet as the paving stones rushed up to meet him.

"Aye, man, and that's a nasty one all right," a soft Scots-Irish voice burred near Andrew's ear. He flinched as the ointment the man was applying stung his wound. "Easy now. Ye've a fine gash there, but it'll heal."

Andrew opened his eyes. His skull was being bandaged by a handsome man with a broad forehead, wavy hair, and clear gray eyes.

"Malcolm, Dr. Andrew Malcolm," his attendant introduced himself. "I must say, you don't seem the sort to be brawling."

The object of his frenzied hunt returned to Andrew. "Wilma!" He started to jump up but was overcome with dizziness.

A firm hand on his shoulder pushed him back.

"Just sit a minute until your head clears. You'll be right soon."

"My friend. I must warn her—the epidemic—" But he calmed and told Dr. Malcolm about his chase to keep the ladies from exposing themselves to danger.

The doctor nodded. "Aye. Ye're right about keeping away. The papers understate it—don't want to start a panic. We're faced with no mere epidemic. This is a plague. Mark my words, this will be a plague in comparison with which all previous pestilence will seem trivial and insignificant."

He paused. "Unless Almighty God in His wisdom chooses to spare us."

Andrew struggled to his feet. It didn't seem that the Infinite Wisdom had chosen to spare them much of anything.

CHAPTER EIGHT

It was late afternoon before Andrew could attempt driving the ten miles home. They would probably be finished at the soup kitchen now. What had happened? Had Wilma returned safely? Or had she and Mrs. Foxe been caught in the riot? Had they failed in their errand to purchase grain? Was the kitchen even able to open?

He attempted whipping his horses to a trot. But the road was as congested as it had been that morning, and now traffic was moving even more slowly. The people hungrier, more fatigued.

In spite of the few starvelings sitting on the pavement, a pall of desertion hung around the warehouse soup kitchen as if it had never been open. Heavy with weariness, weighted down by the very hopelessness in the air, Andrew hitched his team and shuffled to the door, dreading the news he must face.

To his surprise, the door opened readily. And there she was, wearing her deep purple dress with a white apron over it, her dark hair curling around her face.

Wilma took one look at him, dropped her broom, and rushed to him with her hands out. "Oh, Andrew! My dear. What has happened to you?" She put a careful finger to the bandage. "You're hurt. Come, sit down."

It was not his injury that made his knees weak but the relief of seeing her. He sat. "I went to Belfast. To warn you. Selma said—"

"Belfast? We didn't go to Belfast. Merely to Newtownards."

He gripped the edge of the bench for support. "I can't tell you how thankful I am to hear that. The epidemic—plague, they're saying now—Wilma, you can have no notion of the horror—people lying dead on the street—" He straightened up and grabbed her shoulders. "Wilma, you must not go near it. I want you to give up the soup kitchen work."

She gasped in protest, but he hurried on. "You are too dear to me. There are others who can do this work. You must not expose yourself." He took her hands. "My love, I've been slow to speak of so many things. But today when I thought I might not find you again, when I was surrounded by such horror, I determined that, if God would give me a second chance, I wouldn't delay. You must cease this work. And you must marry me."

After a moment's hesitation, Wilma let out a trill of laughter. "Yes. Yes, Andrew, that is exactly what we must do. Not quit the kitchen—we'll talk about that. But we must marry. I saw that this morning, too. It's as if—" she hesitated, then pressed on, "as if we are living in the midst of a dread, silent devastation that's harder to fight than the hunger itself. But we must fight. And we can be stronger together."

It was fortunate they were alone in the room, for nothing could have stopped Andrew's taking his beloved into his arms at that moment.

They were driving toward Harrowby's Dale, Wilma's bonneted head resting on his shoulder, when she said, "See, it's as if things are somehow better already, isn't it? I don't mean just for us—but it's as if I can give the new hope I feel to others. We can beat it—this—this unseen ruin creeping around us."

"Yes. We can. We will." He smiled tenderly at her. Somehow, just in the time since they had declared their love, she had become infinitely more precious to him.

She sighed and snuggled a hand under his arm. "I saw it all so clearly today in Newtownards. It was so awful in the workhouse. I asked about that family we took in. The little boy is the only one still liv—"

"What?" Andrew jerked his team to such an abrupt halt they were almost thrown from the seat. "You went to the workhouse!"

"Why, yes. It's part of the Friends' program—to take comfort to—"

"No, Wilma. No!" he exclaimed, as if he could change the facts by denying them.

"I know—I had hoped for better news, too. The mother and her babes dead. A small defeat in the face of so much death. But forgive me—I did not want to talk of defeat tonight. Tonight we are to hold the doom at bay."

Andrew shook his head against the crush of inevitability. He had struggled to protect her, but his best efforts were less than the wind. When she bade him good night in the hall, her eyes were so bright. Then the darkest thought of all struck him. Were they fever-bright?

And then the situation that could get no worse got worse. Several shiploads of Irish emigrants were turned back from Glasgow and other British cities. Regardless of where they had come from, all were dumped into the most convenient port—Belfast.

Fourteen thousand people crowded Belfast's hospitals and workhouse. Hundreds, for whom no provision could be found, huddled on the streets. Dr. Malcolm reckoned for the *Belfast News Letter* that one out of every five persons in the city was infected with plague. "In the delirium of this frightful malady they are left exposed in the streets or abandoned to die in their filthy, ill-ventilated hovels," the doctor concluded.

Fever penetrated every part of Ulster. Public works closed down. Soup kitchens struggled to continue with less than half their volunteers. Many finally shut their doors, leaving the starving, fevered victims to die clutching their empty bowls.

The plague reached its peak in July. On the first day of August, Wilma died.

Perhaps the worst of it was that Andrew could not mourn. All human passion had withered. He knew that was the end—there was no feeling, no meaning to anything. There was no food for his soul hunger. Physical hunger could be fed with wheatmeal. But the hunger he'd thought could be fed with love mocked any attempt at satisfaction.

His love lay in the grave. And famine in the heart was more severe than any in the stomach. There was no food for the hunger he felt. If there was nutrition that could give meaning to life, how was it that the further he searched, the hungrier he became?

Or perhaps that was the answer—merely to hunger on until one reached the void.

Or maybe this was the void.

Maybe they were all dead.

Dead. And in hell.

CHAPTER NINE

The old saying had been "To hell or to Connacht." Bridget's ancestors had chosen Connacht. But was there a difference?

She clasped the trug to her chest, enfolding the final digging of her small harvest, and tried to calculate. Did she have fifty pounds? Certainly, the small mound in the lean-to was less than a hundredweight. In the days before the famine, Dermot alone would have eaten this many tatties in two weeks. But now it must keep them both for a whole year.

The autumn of 1847 had yielded its harvest. The potatoes—what few there were—were sound. The fever epidemic had run its course, and the government had declared the famine officially over. How could it be over when people were still starving—the workhouses still overflowing—the destitute still dying on their doorsteps? Yet, the government said it was over and halted its distribution of soup. Two months earlier, three million people had been fed by government ration tickets. Now there were no more tickets. And no more soup.

Bridget turned to stow her basket of brown diamonds. A hairless brown dog wandered across the field, its backbone protruding like the teeth of a saw. It glared at her with a wolfish eye, then slunk away. The birds that had twittered last spring sang no more. The soul of the land was faint and dying.

Dermot had said that. It was rhetoric from his Young Irelander meetings. But maybe they weren't so far wrong. Dying. Or already dead.

She selected two large potatoes and one small one and went into the hut. She would boil them for dinner. They could drink the cooking water for supper. Inside the door, she froze.

She hadn't thought it possible to feel a new fear, but the sight of Dermot gathering his few belongings into a woven rush basket stabbed like a knife through her heart.

"Dermot, no! I've tatties. A whole mound. We've enough. There's no need for you to leave." In her desperation she lied, pouring out words neither of them believed. "We've made it this far. Don't emigrate now. The ships are death pits—better to go directly to the trench in the churchyard."

He gripped her arm and shook her until she stopped on a sob. "Wheesht, woman! Who'd have thought ye had the energy to set up such a howl?"

"But—"

"I'm not taking ship. I'm going to Dublin."

She sank to the pallet where *Seanathair* lay, hollow-eyed and cadaverous, hardly making a ridge under the brychan. She voiced what she knew her grandfather was too weak to say. "As well take a coffin ship, then. There is nothing in Dublin. No land for crops, no space in the workhouse, not even kelp to boil—"

Dermot wrinkled his nose against the seaweed smell permeating the cabin. "Aye. If I wanted kelp would I go to Dublin?"

"But what's in Dublin?"

"The future."

"There is no future."

Now the bitterness that had sustained Dermot in the worst moments surged in his speech. "You talk like all the others. Like the Irish have always done when they didn't have someone to lead them." Bridget sighed. She had heard it all too many times before. "O'Connell's dead, Dermot. Let him rest."

"O'Connell! Aye, rest. That's all he did at the end, anyway."

"He won emancipation for us."

"Oh, aye. The Great Liberator. He earned the title well enough. Then turned around and bargained with the enemy."

"It's not the time for a rising, Dermot." If anything could make her think it might be better for her brother to emigrate it was talk of a rising.

"But the time is coming. Soon. Next year is forty-eight.

Fifty years since Wolfe Tone's rising. Time indeed. Time to break this fiendish union with Britain."

She could only shake her head. She had no more strength for arguing. The rock crushing, building roads to nowhere, had taken every ounce of mental and physical energy from the men who were left. Now when they met at the crossroads, it was with empty hands. So they talked of the Brotherhood of Young Ireland—because talk was all they had.

Daniel O'Connell had died last spring, while making a pilgrimage to Rome to pray for Ireland. But his break with the Young Irelanders had been complete before that. Now the way was clear for those calling for the taking up of sword and pitchfork. The spirit of Wolfe Tone walked the pages of *The Nation* and made its way into the hearts of those who could read or who would listen to it read aloud.

"We've a new leader. Smith O'Brien, descendant of Brian Boru. He's visionary enough to see clearly through the film of suffering encasing this land. New ties have been forged in the fires of the famine. If anything good can have come of this, it's that the horror has effected a purge in the gentry. Attitudes have changed. Attitudes hard as iron can be hammered on the anvil of freedom."

At such moments, Dermot displayed his descent from a long line of *seanchaidhs*. And there was no arguing with him once the poetry rose.

Bridget got up wearily. "I'll cook extra tatties for ye to eat on the road." She calculated how many *Seanathair* was likely to need. She could send the rest with Dermot. She had raised them for him.

It was as well, she considered. She had not told Dermot that the few pecks of barley she sold had paid only half the rent. But Dermot would go to Dublin with his Young Irelanders, and there would be enough potatoes and paid-up rent to last until she took *Seanathair* to the churchyard. Then she would go to the workhouse. Unless she was lucky and the fever took her farther away.

She took the St. Bridget's cross from the wall just inside the door and placed it on the top of his bundle. "The God of St. Patrick and Ireland watch over you, Dermot."

"And may the same God watch over you."

That winter was the coldest yet. There were deep snows in February. What if *Seanathair* died now? Who could dig a grave in such rock-hard ground? As the old man's breath came more shallow and ragged, Bridget found herself more and more obsessed with the thought. The mortal remains of generations of MacHenrys rested in the churchyard. She would not have the finest of them tipped into a famine pit. Perhaps, if he could just hold on a bit longer… the thaw must come soon.

That was all she cared about. Her final goal would be reached then, and she could give up the struggle. In spite of everything, she managed a smile. She had done it. A handful of small potatoes remained in the basket. Brendan MacHenry would die with his own thatch over his head.

He would be laid out and waked by his own granddaughter. Father Lynch would lay him in St. Finian's churchyard…

And then? Her plan had been to go to the workhouse. But too many had sought their last refuge there. If the snows went off soon enough, it would be better to stay here and eat grass. Many had chosen to die with a green mouth in the open field rather than with fever in the poorhouse. Perhaps she would make that choice as well.

Several days later she lay on her pallet, thinking the same thoughts round and round, except that the thoughts came less clearly now. Often she didn't know whether she slept or daydreamed, whether it was day or night. It made no difference. She would listen for *Seanathair's* breath, then sink back into her stupor.

But this time she did not sink back. There had been a sound, and it was not *Seanathair*. It was a knocking. She dragged herself to the door.

"Father Lynch. You're good to come."

"Bless you, daughter. And how is himself?"

It had become a ritual. And at every visit she had replied, "He breathes." But tonight, she said, "Have you your stole, Father?"

"Indeed, I have. It's time, is it?"

She nodded.

The priest took his purple stole out of his pack, kissed it, put it over his shoulders and knelt by the barely breathing form. He made the sign of the cross. "God the Father—"

Bridget gave the response, "Have mercy on your servant."

"God the Son—"

"Have mercy on your servant."

"God the Holy Spirit—"

"Have mercy on your servant."

"Holy Trinity, one God—"

"Have mercy on your servant."

"Jesus, Lamb of God—"

"Have mercy on him."

"Jesus, bearer of our sins—"

"Have mercy on him."

"Jesus, Redeemer of the world—"

"Give him your peace."

Father Lynch placed a crumb of the host on the tongue that had once sung so fair to make children dance and men weep. "Lord, have mercy."

"Christ, have mercy."

"Lord, have mercy."

Bridget had no idea how long she sat there after Father Lynch left. Perhaps she dozed. Or perhaps the cabin actually grew warm with a soft light. Perhaps a breeze or a moth's wing ruffled the strings of Brendan MacHenry's harp. Or perhaps the angels really sang a heavenly welcome for the *seanchaidh*. But whatever the truth of the matter, Bridget knew it was time.

She moved slowly but with determination. She must find the strength for this one last thing. Tugging with both hands, she pulled the table to the center of the room. That task done, she found strength for the next and went to the small trunk in the corner. She was glad she had kept it— her grandmother's wedding veil. Many a time she had thought of trying to sell it. She would have offered it for rent had *Seanathair's* breath outlasted her final payment. But that had not been necessary. She covered the table with the fragile lace, then turned to bathe the body, more frail than even the veil.

She had washed his shirt and dried it by the fire only last week. His hair and beard lay smooth under the furrows of the comb. She had no candles, but she had been careful never to be without a supply of rushes. Now she lit one to place in the window and one for the holder on the shelf. The light flickered on the silvery hair and ivory lace, giving an otherworldly atmosphere to the scene. Bridget would not have been surprised if *Seanathair's* body had simply floated to paradise with the soul that had already departed.

She knelt by the side of the table. "O God, whose only begotten Son, by His life, death, and resurrection has purchased for us the rewards of eternal life…"

Bridget blinked at the morning light when Father Lynch pushed open the cabin door. She remembered that *Seanathair* was gone. There was nothing left. Nothing in the whole world. "There are three potatoes in the basket, Father. You must give them to the poor." She would not be needing them. Grandfather's bones would go in the pit today. Perhaps she could just lie there with him when no one was looking. It would save their having to carry her from the field.

Father Lynch signed Brendan MacHenry's forehead, lips, and heart with the cross, then turned to Bridget. "You have done well, my child. He looks fine."

"Aye. He was always beautiful. But, no—" the old worry gripped her with the return of the full light of day. "No, you cannot take him yet. He must have his own grave." She looked around wildly. "My loy. It's sturdy. I can dig the grave."

"No, child. You—"

"Father Lynch, I can. I can. Seanathair mustn't go in the pit. I can do it. The ground can't be frozen that hard. I —I'll—"

The old priest grasped her shoulders to calm her, and she slumped against him. "Go calmly, my child. There's no need."

She tried to struggle but was too spent.

"The digging's been done. By his own kin."

"Dermot?" She looked around. "Dermot's come back? Oh, thank You, Jesus, Mary, and Saint Patrick."

But the figure who entered the cabin just then was not her brother. She shrank behind the priest at the sight of a stranger in black coat and crepe armbands.

"Aye, it's little wonder that ye nae recognize me, Bridget MacHenry. We're sore changed, all of us. Ye'll ken that I said I'd return. I'd no notion it would be under such circumstances, though."

Father Lynch put an arm around Bridget. "He says his

name is Andrew Armstrong, come from County Down. He said he was kin. I'd no reason to doubt him."

Bridget nodded. "Aye. It was the shock. It's as he says." She made a weak gesture for the men to sit on the bench and all but collapsed on her pallet. "It's been long."

Andrew nodded. "Aye. Several lifetimes." And silence filled the space between each word. "I've come with the Quakers. They set up boilers—run soup kitchens. The government quit; so many landlords are bankrupt; but the Quakers carry on."

She looked at his sober attire. "So, you've become one of these—these—what?"

"No. No, I'm not anything. Not anymore." The sadness in his voice was like the mourning of the sea.

While they talked, Father Lynch busied himself poking up the turfs, filling a kettle with water, and boiling the last potatoes.

Andrew explained that when the Friends Relief Committee received a shipment of boilers and supplies from England, they decided to send them to the west where the need was the greatest. "Mrs. Amelia Foxe, the valiant lady in charge—a right dynamo she is—is after being a friend of mine." His face darkened. "We've been through the deep times together." He paused.

Bridget thought it sounded like he choked, but he cleared his throat and hurried on. "I had a mind to make good on my promise to return, so I offered to drive her in my wagon. We'll be in the area a few days, making deliveries to volunteers." He rushed to the end of his explanation, then fell silent.

Bridget nodded. A few days. Then she must go on living a few days more. Then a worse thought struck her. If there was to be a soup kitchen in their village, she must eat. To refuse would be to commit suicide. And suicide was a sin. But she didn't want to go on living. Why couldn't Andrew Armstrong have waited just a few more days? Then it wouldn't have mattered if manna had fallen from heaven. She would not have been obliged to stir herself to eat it for fear of her immortal soul.

Was even such a thought sin?

"Eat this in remembrance of him."

She obediently opened her mouth. Then she realized Father Lynch was holding out a potato, not serving the holy eucharist. Yes, she would eat in *Seanathair's* memory. She would need strength for the funeral.

Father Lynch and Andrew Armstrong wrapped Brendan MacHenry in his brychan and placed him in the coffin that Andrew brought in from his wagon.

Bridget's mouth fell open when she saw it. "How…?"

"Mrs. Foxe wanted to talk to the priest about setting up the soup kitchen. That's when I met Father lynch, and he told me…" Andrew glanced at the body laid out so lovingly on the table. "I fetched it then. There are plenty—so few can afford them now…" He stumbled to a halt, as if he realized he was babbling.

Bridget sat with a dazed look on her face. It dawned on her slowly that a miracle was taking place. The digging of the grave was enough. She had never even thought of a coffin. But Jesus—or Mary—or the fairies had sent Andrew with a fine pine coffin as well. She made no attempt to hold back the tears.

Bridget jostled between Andrew and Father Lynch as the wagon lumbered over the frozen ruts and the coffin bounced in the back. But to her the ride seemed as smooth as a flight of angels' wings.

Piles of snow still lay on the shaded side of St. Finian's churchyard, but she did not feel the cold. She stood beside the fresh-turned mound as the men lowered the coffin.

Father Lynch held his prayer book. "A reading from a sermon by Saint Anastasius of Antioch. 'To this end Christ died and rose to life that He might be Lord both of the dead and of the living. But God is not God of the dead, but of the living. That is why the dead, now under the dominion of one who has risen to life, are no longer dead but alive. Therefore life has dominion over them and, just as Christ, having been raised from the dead, will never die again, so too they will live and never fear death again.'"

CHAPTER TEN

The words entered Andrew's dulled brain. *So too they will live and never fear death again.* He supposed something like that had been said at Wilma's funeral, but he had been too numb to hear. Now he listened more closely.

"'When they have been thus raised from the dead and freed from decay, they shall never again see death, for they will share in Christ's resurrection just as He Himself shared in their death.'"

The words brought a tinge of warmth to his frozen heart. Even if they weren't literally true, they made beautiful poetry. The very concept that hope could exist in religion or art was in itself hopeful.

The service continued, but now Andrew did not resist it as the frozen earth had resisted his digging that morning. He let the words float around him as he would a *seanchaid's* tale, as he had once listened to Brendan MacHenry.

"Concerning those who are asleep, do not be sad like men who have no hope…"

Bridget nudged him, indicating that he should join her in the response. "For if we believe that Jesus died and rose again, God will bring forth with Jesus all who have fallen asleep believing in him."

"Do not weep for the dead, do not mourn them with tears."

This time Andrew listened to his own response from the book Father Lynch had put in his hand before the service began. "For if we believe that Jesus died and rose again, God will bring forth with Jesus all who have fallen asleep believing in him." A pretty big if, but still—nice words.

They were nearly back to the cabin when Andrew heard clangs and thuds coming from the MacHenry hut. Two uniformed, helmeted constables blocked the way to the door. Three ragged laborers swung sledgehammers and a battering ram at the stones and turf that had housed generations of MacHenrys.

Bridget gave a piercing cry, such as she might have been expected to emit at her grandfather's grave, then, just as suddenly, returned to her dazed silence.

"Here now! What's this?" Andrew jumped from the wagon seat with a shout.

A pinched-looking man in a tweed cap confronted him. "Grady Erskine. Lord Grangeton's overseer," he announced himself. "Rent past due. Thought they'd cleared out. Save us the trouble of throwing them out. But I read the eviction notice anyway. The constable here will swear to it. Things always done by the letter of the law on Lord Grangeton's land."

"I've no doubt." Andrew had no trouble matching the hardness in Erskine's voice.

The overseer drew a crumpled paper from his back pocket. "'Hear ye, hear ye. The queen's business is now in progress, to ensue forthwith, and not to be interfered with—'"

Andrew pushed the paper aside. "You've no need to read the riot act to me, man. I've no intention of interfering with you or Her Majesty. But Lord Grangeton owns only this cabin and the land it's on. If his lordship is so careful about the letter of the law, you'll be knowing that the tenants' personal property is theirs to take." He advanced toward the door as he spoke, and the constabulary moved aside.

Andrew's shoulders slumped. It had been a small victory. But what could there be in this hovel worth taking away? He started to take Bridget's brychan, then considered that it would inevitably be full of lice. He chose the empty potato basket instead. The two iron rushlight holders went in, the bit of lace on which the mortal remains of Brendan MacHenry had lain, the St. Bridget's cross from beside the fireplace. "To save the hearth from fire and ravagement," she had said in lighter days. It hadn't worked.

He was ready to leave when he saw the harp in a shadowed corner. He picked it up and ran his fingers over the satiny black wood. Then he strode to the rig and placed the treasure in Bridget's lap.

Even before he was on the wagon seat again, Erskine signaled his men, and the blows resumed on the cabin walls.

But now it was not only the pounding of battering ram on stone that accompanied their departure but also the silver warble of Bridget's fingers on the harpstrings.

He looked at her in amazement. "I didnae know ye played!"

"I didn't. *Seanathair* showed me. And now the gift is passed. It is only for its owner that the *cláirseach* sings its true sweetness."

"And did your grandfather teach you his songs as well?" It had all been long ago, on the other side of the famine wall, that long-ago time and place when life had been good and sweet and filled with song. And he had asked Bridget to gather songs for him.

"Aye. I had no paper. So, I got them by heart."

Andrew looked at the child on the seat beside him, clutching the few possessions that were all she had in the world. What was he to do with her? She had said Dermot was somewhere in Dublin—gone off to join the Young Irelanders. Should he take her to her brother? Enough careful questioning in pubs should unearth his whereabouts —if he hadn't already gotten himself jailed or knifed in some sectarian squabble.

The answer was easy enough for tonight. Father Lynch

had offered Andrew hospitality. His first impulse had been to refuse—surely there would be an inn, however mean, in a nearby town. But now he was glad he had accepted. When the priest learned Bridget had been evicted, he would give her a sleeping place as well. And perhaps for longer than tonight, Andrew mused. Perhaps she could serve as housekeeper for the elderly priest. Yes, that would be a fine solution. He clucked to his team with renewed spirit.

Andrew's optimism lasted until he saw the priest's home. It was barely more than a hermit's cell, built in the ancient style with cobblestones stacked to form a steeply pitched roof. But it was warm and dry and there was room —barely—for the three of them to sleep on brychans before the fire.

Father Lynch went straight to the question when they told him of the eviction. "And what will you do now, my child?"

It was obvious from Bridget's widened eyes that she had given the matter no consideration. "I—I don't know. I had thought to die when I'd buried *Seanathair*. Now..." The barrenness in her voice filled the space.

At least, Andrew knew what he was to do for the next few days. "I have a list, Father—of the places the Society of Friends want to start soup kitchens. I'm to deliver the supplies. Their workers will arrive soon—mostly on foot, I expect. Anyway—" he drew a sheet of paper from his pocket. "Could you give me directions to some of these? The villages on the top of the list are on my map." He took out the crumpled document. "But I can't locate some of the others."

Father Lynch studied the list by a flickering rushlight. "Yes, your journey is well organized for you." He traced the path on Andrew's map. "These two are quite near—you can be there by midmorning tomorrow. But Finn Birne is being a piece farther on."

As he talked, Andrew jotted notes of landmarks.

"Aye, it's rough going here, the descent very steep. I'd not attempt it myself except on foot, but—" Father Lynch spread his hands. "I'll ask St. Patrick to give you special protection on your mission of mercy."

The priest frowned before going on. "There are people there who've had naught but seaweed and mussels for three years. If they're still alive…" He paused at the last name on the list. "Inish Malin. Aye. You'll be hiring a boat, then. See you set out in fine weather. If it's not too blustery or the mists too heavy, you'll do."

Andrew was not encouraged by the tone of doubt in the cleric's voice. He looked to see how much Bridget had taken in of their conversation and saw that she had none of it. She slept curled before the fire. In the dim room with the fire glow on her, the dirt and ravages of the past years were softened. He could see glimmers of the red-gold child who had once entranced him with her bell-like laughter. Her vulnerability and aloneness struck him anew.

He saw that Father Lynch observed the direction of his gaze. "I'll take her with me, Father. She can stay in one of the villages with the Quakers. They can give her soup, and she can give them songs. This will be something new for even as advanced a group as the Society of Friends—a soup kitchen with a *seanchaidh*."

Having arrived at that happy solution, Andrew settled himself as comfortably as he could for the night. Rolling in a brychan on a beaten earth floor was all very well for people accustomed to such things. But Andrew Armstrong was not. He smiled at the thought of Grandfather seeing him now. Jay Lanark had been irate at his leaving. But that made little enough difference to Andrew. Nothing had made any difference since Wilma's death. So why shouldn't he take soup boilers to the west coast? One place was as empty as another.

And now he had another chore. He would deliver Bridget along with the kitchen supplies. And then he would return to the emptiness of Lanarks' Bawn.

CHAPTER ELEVEN

The next day, when he explained his decision to Bridget, she neither objected nor stated acquiescence. She merely stored her rolled brychan neatly against the wall and ate the small bowl of stirabout the priest set before her.

Andrew left a bag of meal with the priest, and they set out. The first two villages were as easy to find as his guide had assured him they would be. But the plague and fever had found them equally accessible. A few destitute beings leaned against run-down huts with scanty thatch. Andrew would hardly have thought to dignify the decrepit collection of sticks and stones with the title of clachan, much less village, in spite of the presence of the requisite smithy and dram shop. Leaving Bridget in either place was unthinkable. They rattled on.

The trail grew steeper and rougher. As they crossed the Black Gap, Andrew recalled Father Lynch's admonition that this land was best crossed on foot, and he hoped that the meager track wouldn't peter out on them. By evening, though, they were descending with a view of Donegal Bay spread before them. This looked better. Surely Bantooley would be just the place to establish Bridget along with the soup boiler.

And perhaps it would have been, as it was a somewhat larger village that boasted its own church. But the Quaker workers had not arrived yet, so the equipment must be left with the priest. And Andrew would not—could not—leave his young cousin without speaking to the Quakers in whose care he meant to leave her.

And so, they went on.

On the second day she asked shyly, "Should I be teaching you the songs so you'll have them when you go?"

Andrew sighed. The publishing of songbooks was something else the world had left on the other side of the famine wall. But these were some of the first words Bridget had volunteered since they departed from Grangeton. It would be as well to encourage her.

"I would be happy to hear them." He tried to put a bit of enthusiasm into his words.

Her light melodies did not smooth the roads, but it seemed that the horses stumbled less on the ruts. And Andrew realized how much he had missed the presence of music in the world. In the old days—days before the Great Hunger—he had occasionally gone to church with Grandfather. Although the metrical psalms were monotonous to his ears, they were music. And there had been harpers and fiddlers and pipers at fairs. And children had sung in the fields and clachans. He had forgotten the sound of it all.

And the birds had sung! Those few birds that had survived the harshness of the winters and escaped trapping for food had faced their own famine as the earth was wiped clear of berries, seeds, and even bugs—all scoured for human consumption.

But here, for this brief space, there was melody in the air. Andrew consulted his map. The last place was an island. That should be perfect for a *seanchaidh*: green, with sandy coves and wild, rocky outcrops. A place with ancient memory of legendary *selkies* and water fairies.

Yes. It was a good thing none of the other villages had suited. Inish Malin would do far better.

Three days later they arrived at the westernmost tip of the peninsula, where Donegal Bay faced the open waters of the Atlantic. The dark mound of an island showed offshore, silhouetted by the setting sun.

Andrew approached a party of wrackers gathering seaweed on the shore. "Can you tell me, is that Inish Malin? Where can I get a boat to ferry us out there?"

Sticklike children hid behind their mothers' tattered skirts. A young boy made a sign against evil. A girl fled, screaming.

Bridget touched his arm. "They aren't understanding yourself."

She turned and spoke to them in a lilting flow of Irish.

The children came out from hiding. A stooped old man gave a few words of reply.

Bridget nodded and spoke a few more words in Irish, then turned back to Andrew. "Aye, it's for being Inish Malin. But they have no boats. Fishing isn't allowed them. Lord Malinmore keeps the boats."

Bridget helped a small girl struggling with a basket of kelp while Andrew considered what they should do. He had hoped to make his last delivery tomorrow and start home—although the thought of going home to the gray emptiness of the world without Wilma was not enticing. Except for the comfort of his bed, there was little to choose between Father Lynch's cell and Lanarks' Bawn.

He looked at his map. They were twenty miles from Glenties. They could go there tomorrow. He had often heard the Glenties Union talked of at relief committee meetings. Run by the British Association, they fed eight thousand children a week. Surely, they could use an additional boiler and another willing worker—for he did not doubt that Bridget would be willing. That was a better choice than some unreachable island. If he couldn't get there, then neither could the Quakers. They had probably gone on to Glenties as well. On that decision, he folded his map.

But before he could announce his new plan, Bridget tugged at his arm. "Come. This way."

He would have demanded an explanation, but she returned to her Irish jabber with the people, who began escorting the newcomers down the beach.

At the shore, all but one fell back. "Desmond—Des," a

black-haired youth introduced himself. It appeared that he would be their guide to somewhere.

But where? Andrew hesitated at leaving his horse, wagon, and the soup boiler unguarded. These people looked desperate enough to attempt eating his horse. He had a fleeting vision of horseflesh roasting over the broken boards of his cart.

"The *seanathair* will guard it." Bridget spoke as if she had read his mind.

Ashamed of his thoughts, yet relieved, Andrew nodded and followed.

At the coastline, the sand gave way to a shale-covered path that grew more and more rugged until Andrew feared he would lose his footing and slip into the water. Suddenly it appeared that was what Des had done, for his dark head vanished from sight. A moment later, however, Andrew followed the sharp turn in the trail and saw that their guide had merely ducked into a cave in the side of the cliff. And there lay a sturdy rowboat.

Bridget explained. "People have hidden boats here since the time of Cromwell, when all the priests were driven out. They spirited priests to Inish Malin and slipped them back under cover of dark to say the Mass. When the potatoes failed, they fished at night." She shrugged. "It was little enough to choose—death from the law for fishing without rights or death from hunger by not fishing."

Andrew would have preferred to wait till morning, but Desmond would take the boat out only under cover of dark.

He should go back and get the boiler and supplies he was to deliver—in case the Quakers were there, ready to set their kettles boiling. But the thought of traversing that trail again— and the return laden with a heavy boiler—made him decide to go ahead and just make the arrangements. He would bring back one of the islanders to take over the equipment if the Quakers hadn't their own boat. Yes. He nodded to himself and got into the small, rocking craft. That would do very well. Get Bridget settled in her new home. Best to do that first.

The pale half-moon gave only a cold light, and the few stars showing served to highlight the blackness around them. When they reached the island shore, the dark seemed thicker yet.

Through Bridget, Andrew had asked about the island's population and was told there were more than a hundred the last anyone knew. But that had been some time ago, as no one had come from the island during the winter storms.

Andrew felt a prickle at the back of his neck. It was too dark. Even with the village asleep, there should have been a glow from banked fires or a wavering rushlight indicating some sleepless soul.

He jumped when a marsh bird, startled from its nest, flew low over his head, crying.

Bridget moved closer. "Des says we must leave before sunrise."

"Nonsense. I paid him more than his whole village has

seen in a year. I need to talk to these people—have you talk to them, at least."

Unless there was an educated priest on the island, this was going to be more awkward than Andrew had imagined. And he had no intention of tackling such obstacles in the dark. The only thing he would undertake before daylight would be finding a protected spot to doze. Fortunately, he had a few brimstone matches in the little tin box in his pocket.

But even when they crowded around a small blaze built at the foot of a standing stone above the beach, he mostly had only disgust to keep himself warm. Disgust with himself. How could he have gotten into such an awkward situation? It was more than awkward. And more than disgust with the dark, the isolation, the language barrier, the penetrating cold. He couldn't define it, but as he huddled deeper inside his voluminous MacFarlan coat, he began to feel an eeriness creeping over him.

Something was… wrong. He hesitated to use the word "evil," and yet he could think of nothing better. And Bridget? What of his plan to abandon her here?

But he wasn't abandoning her. He was bringing her to a new home. A place of beauty and poetry, where she could run free in the grass and play her harp by the seaside. Of course, he was. It would all look better in the morning.

He must have dozed in spite of his agitation, because a rim of gold was gilding the sky to the east when he opened his eyes.

For their breakfast he had only a few hard biscuits in

his pocket, left over from supper last night. It was unlikely they could buy food in the island village, but he would try. When he set out on this journey he had no idea of the isolation—or desolation—of such villages as their journey had taken them to in recent days. And there was little to be hoped for from this island unless the Quakers had established their work ahead of him.

He looked across the expanse of open green. He should have known better than to expect animals in the fields. If ever there had been any, they would have been eaten in the first year of the famine. Yet it seemed something should be moving. The stillness had a breathless quality despite the breeze blowing in from the sea.

How would people have fared here? he wondered. Notwithstanding the Irish dependence on and preference for potatoes, there should have been no shortage of fish. Could they have survived all these years on fish and seaweed alone? He looked around. Wind-ruffled grass was the only thing that told him he wasn't beholding a painted scene. There was no sign of tilled soil. Still, it was a week or so yet till St. Patrick's Day—they probably wouldn't start digging until the traditional time.

Bridget came up from the shore. He was pleased to see that she had washed herself. That was a good sign. She was coming back to life and making ready to settle into her new home. Des refused to leave his boat, so Andrew held his hand out to Bridget and the two of them climbed the winding path to high ground, where scattered stone buildings stood well away from the shore.

The closer they drew to the buildings, the more his nervousness increased. What if the Quakers weren't here yet? What would he do with Bridget? The language was no problem to her, but he couldn't leave her in an isolated, starving village without the protection of a charitable society. And he had no desire to spend more time here than necessary, awaiting the others' arrival.

Bridget seemed to feel none of his reluctance. She almost skipped ahead of him on the path. Even in the few days of eating the proper food Andrew had brought, she had gained strength. And today, after her early bath, her hair seemed to have regained some of its original color when the sun shone on it. She stopped before the first cottage. The door stood open.

"Wait!" Andrew wasn't sure why his command was so sharp. He just knew the stillness leaped out to crush him. The silence shrieked.

He pushed open the creaking door and entered. The form on the pallet had been female. It was a mother, clutching the body of a small child.

Andrew clasped a hand over his nose and mouth and backed out, shielding the sight from Bridget behind him. "Don't." He stopped her as she started to move around him. "They're beyond help. We'll go on and find a priest— or someone."

A small stone church stood on up the footpath. Andrew surveyed the churchyard with growing uneasiness. He noted the number of mounds that seemed new since last autumn. The grass had not sodded over them yet. There was a half-dug grave off to the right. Perhaps that was for the woman in the cabin. And yet the dirt around it didn't appear to be new-turned.

Bridget cried out, and he turned to see her pointing. The last shreds of a black cassock told him that the corpse they saw was once a priest. Fallen, too weak to get up, on his way to administer last rites to another, perhaps? The man had been so for some time, for the sea gulls had left little of his face. Andrew put an arm around Bridget and turned her away. "We must go. I must get you away from —from this island of death."

But she did not yield to his movement. "No. We cannot leave." She knelt by the priest, as he had doubtless knelt by so many others. "Our Father…"

Andrew stood stiffly by until she completed the prayer. "Now," he said. "Let's go. This whole place is dead." The enormous horror of the situation had been slowly dawning on him since they arrived at the cove last night. He had known then that something was wrong.

He wasn't a superstitious man. He didn't really believe the dead walked. And yet he looked uneasily over his shoulder. Stone and turf cottages and cabins straggled around in every direction. There were twenty, maybe thirty, buildings, some having little sheds or byres behind them. How many of them were not cottages but tombs? How many of the inhabitants of this once-busy village had received proper burial in the churchyard before the rest simply lay down on their pallets and never found the strength to get up again? The wind made a moaning sound.

Bridget was still kneeling.

"Come." He pulled her to her feet.

"Aye, I was after forgetting myself." She gave a little shake. "Yes, there is so much to do." She started across the churchyard toward another hut.

"Where are you going? The boat is this way."

He might as well have saved his breath. "We must check every cottage. I will say an Ave for each one." She turned back and grabbed his arm, her eyes wide with concern. "Do you think many died without absolution?"

Andrew swallowed his impatience. All he could think of was getting away from this ghastly place. And here she was, worrying about some religious mumbo jumbo. "It appears the priest was the last one on his feet, apparently in the process of preparing a burial. He probably lived long enough to perform—all the necessary rites." He really had no idea, and he couldn't think it would make a whistle of difference. But he was pleased to see that he had said the right thing. The fear in her eyes subsided.

The next few hours were a catalog of horrors. Andrew had no idea where Bridget got her strength—physically or emotionally. She moved steadily from hut to hut, inspecting each interior. When the huts were not empty, when dead eyes looked at them from ragged brychans, when gaping mouths greeted them, she never gave in to fright or disgust but merely crossed herself and knelt at her prayers as calmly as if she were in church.

Andrew, however, did not have the comfort of religious ritual. He saw the dark stains around the corpses where the body fluids had soaked into ragged blankets and dirt floors. He saw the gleam of bones where skin had decomposed. He saw the maggots, the lice, the ants. And he smelled the putrefaction.

Dust thou art, to dust returneth. The phrase ran over and over in his mind. Was this the end of everything—for everyone? Death had looked so much prettier for Wilma, reposing on a lace-edged linen sheet in Harrowby's Dale and laid to rest in the Comber parish churchyard with the reading of the beautiful words of the *Book of Common Prayer*. Even Brendan MacHenry, lying on the table with the rushlight reflecting on his white beard—there had been dignity, an acknowledgment of the human spirit created in the image of God. But this abandoned waste was horror upon horror.

Bridget saw it through to the end. "There." She closed the door on the farthest-out cottage, near to the back side of the island. "There are three men unburied, counting the priest, five women and two little ones." She thought for a moment. "I suppose the babes would weaken and die first, so most would have been buried."

That thought seemed to comfort her, but Andrew was thinking of the nightmare for those last few on their feet. How many of their hundred-some neighbors, friends, and family would they have had to bury? And now it was over for all of them.

The concept of walking out into a black void terrified him. One always thought of life continuing. One cultivated land and built homes and barns for one's posterity; one worked for laws, churches, schools for one's children. But for Inish Malin, the void had descended.

They were more than halfway back across the water to the mainland when Andrew realized that he, at least, did have a future, and therefore he must make plans. Bridget was fully prepared to tell the local priest all that needed seeing to on the island. He must leave word for the Friends workers. Then inspiration struck him. He would leave the boiler and supplies with Desmond. If any people needed a regular nourishing soup it was the wrackers on Donegal Bay. It could keep this village from going the same way Inish Malin had.

But Bridget… He looked at her now. The sea breeze tangled her hair as she told Des about his island neighbors. And Andrew faced the truth that had been growing on him for days. He could never leave her here, the ward of some charity. She was kin. She was part of his past for generations, the past that could make the future live, if they were not all to go the way of Inish Malin.

And suddenly he had the perfect solution. He would take Bridget to Lanarks' Bawn. There was room and enough. Mrs. B could use the help of a pair of young hands. And Elfrith O'Brien could teach her the lessons she had missed in the spotty education of the hedge school. He rather liked the idea of the woman who had mothered him serving as surrogate mother for Bridget as well. That would make them more than cousins. Almost brother and sister.

CHAPTER TWELVE

Andrew, sitting alone at the head of the table—
the place that was now his and had been for the
past blur of years, was hungry. But he had no
idea what he hungered for. Certainly not for another piece
of meat. He pushed away the roast joint surrounded with
vegetables and swimming in gravy.

Berkley tottered in, his head wobbly on his thin neck.
"Shall I pour your port for you now, sir?"

"No, no. I'll get my own."

Andrew jammed his chair back so impatiently that it
slammed against the wall. He wouldn't let Berkley touch
his best liquor—the old coot shook so that he could hardly
hit the glass when he poured. Why hadn't Andrew rid
himself of such incompetence years ago? And Mrs. B too.
His food would be uneatable if Bridget didn't come over
from the clachan daily to keep things at Lanarks' Bawn in
order. He was glad he had brought her here—even if her

coming had sparked his last—and worst—fight with Grandfather.

He strode into the parlor just as the clock on the mantel chimed three. Funny old clock. It had been there forever. Probably came over with St. Patrick. But how could it be so late already? He turned to the sideboard. No, it wouldn't be port. He wanted something stronger. It seemed he did most of the time now.

He poured a full glass, sloshing a little himself, then flung himself onto the dark plush sofa and put his booted feet on the marble-topped table in front of it. He stole a glance at the clock as if to catch the hands in the act of racing ahead.

Eleven years. How was it possible for the wind to blow so fast? People spoke of the sands of time, or of the years running like a river, but Andrew knew better. Sand and water had substance. They could be held in one's hand—no matter how briefly. Their movement could be measured. But time could be held and measured only by the mind of God. He took a deep drink from his glass.

Eleven years ago he had returned from the west, hungry and tired, his senses numbed by the horrors he had encountered. He had brought with him one spark of light in Bridget and her *cláirseach*. And Jay Lanark had thrown her out. "No papists have sullied the portals of Lanarks' Bawn in the near to three hundred years since my ancestor built it. I'll not be the one to let the Devil in now."

Andrew had tried argument. How did Grandfather know what had happened here for two and a half centuries past? It was quite likely there had been more than one Catholic under this roof. The Seaton Court Lanarks had been Catholic—and they were descended from the same ancestors. There were even rumors that the O'Briens—who were welcomed enough as stable hands—had possessed Lanark blood at some time in the past. As did Bridget MacHenry herself. And he wasn't asking Grandfather to adopt the girl—just give her a bed in the servants' quarters and let her earn her keep helping around the house.

As for being "papist," at least Bridget believed in Jesus, whereas Andrew—if he ever stopped to think about it— had his doubts. He had said something of the sort to Grandfather Lanark back then. Now he took another long sip of his drink and closed his eyes to savor the burning sensation in his throat.

The picture that filled his mind was not one to be savored, however. Grandfather's face loomed large, turning red, then white, in Andrew's memory. "She may call herself a follower of Christ, but her allegiance is to the antichrist in Rome!"

Andrew had tried. "But Grandfather, aren't we the ones who say it's not a matter of sacrament or ritual—only a matter of what's in your heart that counts? Aren't we the ones who say it's one's own personal faith that matters? Aren't we the ones who should be willing to listen to the testimony of others?"

"Those in the darkened grip of Rome can have no testimony."

"But—"

"I'll hear no more on it, boy. She goes out."

Andrew had spent his whole life up to that point—nearly twenty-one years—resisting his grandfather. He had always thought that when he came of age he would revolt, claim his inheritance, leave Ireland perhaps. Certainly leave Lanarks' Bawn. But he had just returned from a grueling trip. He was exhausted—physically and emotionally. Was that the night Jay Lanark won?

No, because Andrew had not changed his name or joined the Orange lodge then. Grandfather's victory had been the next year when the old man died and Lanarks' Bawn and his Orange sash passed to Andrew.

It was then that Andrew had begun sitting at the head of the table, and riding around the fields daily, and doing all the things he said he would never do. Somehow, he had become everything he had said he would never be. He could see it in himself, and he hated it in himself, and yet he could not stop himself. And now he was thirty-two, and he might as well be sixty-two. Or eighty-two. It was all the same.

He lunged to his feet and refilled his glass.

The cut crystal bottom was clear of amber liquid when Jay Lanark's gloating countenance appeared again. "You're a Lanark, boy. Just like me."

Andrew threw his glass at the apparition. "No! I'm an Armstrong. And I'll stay Armstrong. You haven't won yet!" For a moment he thought he heard the phantom laugh. Yes, he had managed to defy his grandfather in that one thing. He hadn't changed his name. But he knew it was a hollow victory.

A form appeared at the door. Andrew's hand gripped a cushion to throw, then realized it was Berkley. He was nearly as much of a shade as Grandfather, but still above ground. "Mr. and Mrs. Price, sir."

Andrew came to his feet, wishing he were steadier. "Tammis! So you haven't forgotten your old cousin?"

If Thomas Price had seemed Andrew's junior a few years ago, now it was doubly so. Thomas, with the fair Selma on his arm, was the image of everything Andrew had once hoped for himself.

He waved them to a chair. "Tea, Berkley. Hot and strong." Whether or not his guests felt the need, Andrew certainly did. He turned to the visitors. "How are the children?"

Andrew settled back and awaited the tea that would help clear his head, knowing nothing would be required of him beyond a nod and a smile as Tammis and Selma told the latest accomplishments of nine-year-old Robert, a strapping rider, and seven-year-old Wilma, a budding talent on the pianoforte.

Thomas and Selma had waited the required year of her family's mourning for Wilma and then married as planned. Since then, Thomas had expanded the prosperity of Price's Farm with an ambitious horse breeding program. He now sold thoroughbreds to many of the Anglo-Irish across the island. The little chestnut mare he bought at the Rossheely Fair had dropped some of his best colts.

Andrew once toyed with the notion of undertaking a similar endeavor, but it seemed too much effort. The fields produced well, and he put more land into flax when the linen industry expanded again. Besides, Grandfather had not engaged in breeding as a business enterprise. There. He'd done it again—submitted to the tyranny of the dead. Perhaps that was because he himself was dead. In truth, he had died in the famine, too.

"And Wilma, the clever lass, has begun on her second sampler." Of course, Selma was talking about wee Wilma, not her namesake, but Andrew still caught his breath. How different life might have been if that lovely, laughing girl hadn't died. He found that he struggled now to recapture her image in his mind, but he could still hear the silver chime of her laughter.

Berkley entered with a rattling of teacups. Andrew sprang to take the tray from his hands before it all landed on the floor. "Will you do the honors?" He gestured for Selma to pour out.

Thomas took a long sip of the well-sugared drink his wife handed him. "Ah, lovely." Then he set down his cup with a satisfied sigh. "Sorry we can't stay longer. But we just came by on our way in to Newtownards. Thought you might like to go to the prayer meeting with us."

Andrew frowned. "What prayer meeting?" This was a Monday. Weren't prayer meetings usually held on Wednesdays?

Selma leaned forward, just as he had seen Wilma do so many times. "It's for the revival. So many have feared it might pass us by. The schoolmaster has a real burden for Newtownards. He has started weekly united prayer meetings—and open-airs and cottage gatherings."

"Has he now? I've read there's been a lot of ranting and singing going on. Can't see why folks would want it on their own doorstep, though." Andrew all but scalded his throat with a gulp of tea intended to keep down just such a harsh response as he knew Jay Lanark would have made. "Dashed untidy, that's what it is. Fanatics and imposters." The *Northern Whig* had treated the whole affair with biting sarcasm.

"I'm sorry to hear you feel that way, cousin." Tammis got to his feet and held out a hand to Selma. "We won't bother you further on the subject. But I can assure you the physical manifestations are but a small part—a very small part—of the Spirit's moving. Changed lives, that's what it's all about."

Andrew laughed as he followed them toward the door. "I'll believe that when I see results beyond the sway of emotion. Until then, the only praying I'll do is that the enthusiasts stay away from here."

When his callers were gone, he returned to his chair with such force that he upset his teacup on the side table. He reached for his crumpled newspaper. When Grandfather died, Andrew had no intention of replacing his reading of the more moderate *Belfast News Letter* with the *Northern Whig*, but the *News Letter* subscription ran out first, and he had just gone with things as they were. It was easier that way. It seemed that was the way he made most of his decisions anymore—holding to the line of least resistance.

The headlines screamed at him. "Conviction! Convulsions! Epilepsy! Insanity!" And that was the complimentary part. The paper was reporting events in Ballymena near where the first religious awakenings had taken place in mid-March. Some three thousand Presbyterians, Episcopalians, and Roman Catholics standing in heavy rain had joined in prayer and singing. Many were stricken prostrate in anxiety over their sins, while others knelt in the mud to pray over them.

And thus, it had continued for more than two months. There were daily meetings for praise, prayer, Scripture reading, and exhortation, attracting thousands—and in the busiest time of the year, Andrew thought. When they should be working in their fields, shops, looms, and kitchens. What would all this praying do to commerce? That was what he wanted to know.

Another article quoted a Presbyterian minister from Lisburn, who professed himself to be a good friend of the movement but was nonetheless disturbed over the manifestation of stigmata and other miraculous revelations claimed by some. He explained some of the more ingenious methods of generating these "miraculous" marks, such as writing upon the arm or hand with starch, then rubbing over the area lightly with iodine of potassium.

Andrew muttered over the depths to which people would stoop to gain money or attention—and the avidness with which such antics were greeted by the mob. "I am a believer in the great and glorious Revival," the good reverend had said, "but, since it is as much the duty of a gardener to pluck the weeds as it is his office to plant the flowers, I could not let this fanaticism and imposture to pass."

And rightly so, Andrew thought as he strode from the room, disgusted over all the hubbub. He had delayed far too long over matters of no importance when he should be riding around his fields. Grandfather Lanark would never have waited until the shadows were so long before making his daily inspection tour. Although Cal Dunleer had taken his father's place as overseer, Andrew held firmly to the farmer's foot in the field as being the best manure.

A short time later he was surveying his property with satisfaction. He had put three new fields into flax production this year, and, looking at the rich stand of shoots greening the land, he could tote up the profits in his head.

A few years back, the Ulster linen industry had nearly been wiped out by the cheaper cotton being mass-produced in Britain. And then there was the famine and its subsequent emigration—it was said one million had died and two million had emigrated. The loss of three million workers was the last straw. Wages rose until linen-spinning all but perished. That would have been the end of it had not the industry been rescued from collapse by the appearance of the power loom.

Power loom weaving did, of course, put skilled weavers

out of work, but it was good for the flax-grower, so Lanarks' Bawn again grew flax.

Andrew kicked Fairling to a trot and rounded the hedgerow bordering the field. He was looking across the way to his closest barley field when a feminine voice made his mount shy sideways. Andrew raised his hand to reprimand the horse but halted mid-swing when he saw it was Bridget. Aye, she would be on her way back to the clachan from seeing to the scrubbing in the kitchen. One of the young O'Briens came in to skivvy, but she needed supervision.

"And is it yourself, Andrew Armstrong?" Her smile managed to be sweet and saucy at the same time.

"And who do you think it would be?" He hadn't meant to bark at her, but after the closeness they had shared during the days of death and starvation, the difference in their station always stung him. Sometimes Andrew could almost convince himself those times had been nothing more than a nightmare; that famine, plague, and pestilence had never swept this fair land. But there was Wilma's grave in the churchyard. And here was Bridget, bringing all the memories back with her.

"And isn't it Fairling that I've known from a wane." She stroked the horse's satiny neck. "Ah, but what a fine horse you chose at the Rossheely Fair, Andrew Armstrong. And here's me forgetting myself and stepping out to frighten the creature."

Andrew started to make a noncommittal remark and ride on, but Bridget continued.

"Sure, and I wouldn't have been so wool-gathering, but I was thinking how I should speak to yourself."

"Well, that should be easy enough—you seem to be doing very well right now."

"Aye, but it's not so easy a matter. I would be going to Belfast."

"Belfast? What would you go there for? Is Elfrith needing something?" Even after all these years it rankled him that his old nurse had chosen to marry and move to the clachan when she could have had a place at Lanarks' bawn—although it had proven convenient enough when he needed to place Bridget with the nearby native Irish. "I can get whatever she needs when we take the next load of flax to market—been holding some for the price to rise."

"No, I mean to stay for a time."

"What!" This time it was Andrew's shout that made Fairling shy. It was unthinkable. Who would see to his meals? "Impossible! Mrs. B needs you."

"Mairead O'Brien will help her."

"And what, pray tell, do you think you'll do in Belfast?"

Bridget took a letter from her pocket and handed it up to him. He raised his eyebrows at the fine, crested paper. Paper with the imprint of the Linen Hall Library. Why would anyone be writing to Bridget on stationery like this?

It was from a Mr. Robert Young, a member of the Belfast Society for Promoting Knowledge. He professed himself to be an enthusiast for the collection of Irish music and songs. He had made a careful study of Bunting's Ancient Irish Music, the final version of which had been published nearly twenty years ago. It seemed that in the course of his work he had come upon some tunes of Cashel MacHenry. Somehow, he had traced the relationship to Bridget and wanted to know if she had any more songs.

"What tangled faradiddle is this? You can't be haring off to Belfast to see this Robert Young fellow. You don't know anything about him. I'll reply to this for you. Explain it's impossible."

"It's good of you to offer to trouble yourself, but there's no need. I've already done the replying."

"But that's impossible," he repeated. "You don't write well enough to be corresponding with some chap from the Society for Promoting Knowledge."

"Oh, but Elfrith was after teaching me. And I'm so grateful. It's a fine skill. Still, I'm glad I didn't have the means earlier, or I might not have got the songs by heart from *Seanathair*."

Andrew blinked. Was this the scrap of a child he had brought back from the ravages of death in Connacht? She'd been nothing but hair and bone and large round eyes. How long had it been since he'd seen her? Really seen her—as more than a cog in the household gears that saw to the setting of his meat in front of him? She had filled out remarkably. Her red-gold hair fell halfway to her waist. A memory of her singing stirred.

He thrust the letter back at her. "Aye. I'll be going to market the end of June. You can ride in with me." He spun Fairling around on the narrow path. "And you'll return with me. I'll not leave you with a stranger." He didn't wait for a reply.

Why had the encounter disturbed him so? He should be glad enough to have Brendan MacHenry's songs collected. He had thought of doing something like that himself once. Once—on the other side of the famine wall. Could he ever have been so caught up in music and poetry? It was a good thing he had taken over matters here before he lost all the business sense Grandfather had instilled in him. He used to waste time looking for a meaning to life— for some great answer to the problems of universal suffering and despair. And the answer had been here all the time. Right under his feet. Work. That was the answer.

Grandfather Lanark would be proud. *You're just like me, boy. You're a Lanark.*

This time Andrew didn't chase the shade away. Instead, he smiled at it. So, in the end Jay Lanark was right. And why not? He had been right about everything else.

So be it. Andrew would make the final submission. When he was in Belfast, he would go to see his lawyer. He'd change his name to Lanark. Grandfather's death had allowed him to take over the fields without changing his name. But now the time had come. Let Grandfather have his victory. Let him gloat in his grave. He had little enough else to do there.

CHAPTER THIRTEEN

Andrew couldn't understand why the road to Belfast was so choked with traffic. Wednesday was always a busy market day, but that could hardly explain this crush. His irritation grew as they drew closer to the city. When they came to the bridge, where all the traffic poured inward, he had to wait some time even to get a place in line to cross. It was worse on the other side.

It had been his intention to let Bridget off at the Linen Hall Library and go on, collecting her again when he was finished at the market and with his attorney. This was to be the day Andrew Armstrong would become a Lanark dejure as well as defacto—in law as well as in fact.

And why not have his first name stricken as well? he thought as he waited a chance to turn right out of the flow of traffic. He had never thought much about the fact that his second name was Jay. Bitter laughter rose in his throat.

That was it. Let Andrew Armstrong be dashed. He would become Jay Lanark.

However, there was no question of turning north toward the library. It was as if the globe had tilted and the whole population of Belfast—nae, of Down and Antrim—was being poured into south Belfast. There was nothing to do but follow along.

There was little use even in holding the reins. His team was forced along with the flow. Andrew's grim laughter turned to fury. How dare the fates so conspire against him? What right did all these people have to be going wherever they were going and interfere with his plans?

But Bridget bounced with delight on the seat next to him. "And have you ever seen a finer thing, Andrew Armstrong?"

He wanted to snap at her for calling him that, but he pretended to be absorbed in his non-driving.

Large numbers of people, many of them singing, poured from the Botanic Rail Station. There must have been special trains laid on for this event—whatever it was.

"Wherever so many people are going must be worth seeing," Bridget said. "And just listen to that fine music. Do you know the song?" She began humming along with a jubilant party just emerging into the street ahead of them.

Andrew had to admit that, although he had never heard the tune before, it was catchy. He struggled to comprehend the words. It was something about news—but this could hardly be a conference of journalists. Finally, he sorted out the refrain: "What's the news? Whene'er we meet, you always say—What's the news?"

The carriages moved at about the same pace as the groups on foot, so he had ample time to listen. The song seemed to go on interminably. They must have been on their second time through the ditty when he realized he was listening to a gospel song:

Oh, I have got good news to tell:
My Saviour hath done all things well,
And triumphed over death and hell,

That's the News!

The Lamb was slain on Calvary,

That's the News!

To set a world of sinners free,

That's the News!

And then it dawned on Andrew. This vast crowd—ten thousand, fifteen thousand, maybe more—was funneling into Belfast's Botanical Garden for a mammoth revival rally. And he was stuck in the middle of it.

He observed the people more closely, wondering what fanatics looked like at close hand. Apparently no different from anyone else, unless they were better scrubbed. The throng seemed to be made up of well-dressed, respectable-looking people carrying Bibles and hymn-books. Except for their singing, they were as quiet and orderly as if they were going to meeting. But no Presbyterian would sing such songs in church.

Indeed, Andrew wasn't certain such singing could be truly Christian. It wasn't a metrical psalm. Could God be truly praised in any other voice? Still, he had to admit it wasn't entirely unpleasant.

Bridget, now thoroughly caught up in the spirit of the day, was singing in her clear, lyrical voice, "All hail the power of Jesus' name…" along with a group on the other side of the street.

At the end of Botanic Avenue, drivers were simply leaving their carriages and proceeding on foot to the green sward between the pavilion and the conservatory. Since they were packed in so tightly, the horses could hardly wander off.

There seemed little reason not to follow. As they walked into the garden, Bridget tugged at his arm and pointed upward to the spreading tree branches. "Oh, look, Andrew. The wee wanes are like Zaccheus."

He gave her a blank stare.

"Are ye not knowing the story? Father Lynch told it often—about the man who couldn't see Jesus, so he climbed a tree—"

"Yes, yes, I know the story. But there's little telling what those youngsters will be seeing."

Anything could happen if a crowd this size got out of hand. And from what he had heard of the excesses of other prayer gatherings, Andrew was inclined to expect the worst. Someone thrust a card into his hand. Andrew felt his brows knit in a scowl as he read a printed prayer. *Grant, O God, we beseech Thee, a still greater outpouring of Thy Spirit upon our country and dominions; so as to cause a deep and wide revival of living faith in Christ, working by love and bringing forth all the fruits of the Spirit… Be to our country a wall of fire round about her and the glory in the midst of her.* He crumpled the card.

A man in a black robe with white bands stood on the pavilion steps and held up his hands for silence. The singing stopped, and the vast crowd quieted. The man was introduced as chairman of the meeting, Mr. John Johnston, Moderator of the General Assembly of the Presbyterian Church.

Andrew strained forward. It was all but impossible to hear. As best he could tell, the speaker welcomed them to "this great united prayer meeting which has been arranged to give information about the progress of the revival and to offer prayer for the abundant outpouring of the Holy Spirit." The man voiced praise that across Belfast, and much of the surrounding area, factories and shops had been closed in order to allow people to attend.

Andrew scowled again. Factories closed? On a Wednesday? And what about the spinning of flax—his flax—and the looming of linen? Did they have no orders to fill? Did they not care what happened to flax growers if they let the cotton industry get further ahead of them?

Apparently, they cared more immediately that people be able to hear the proceedings—which few in the wide reaches of the gardens could do. To that end, the crowd was then divided into twenty or so groups, each with its own leader. When things were sorted out, Andrew saw with some relief that the Rev. Mr. Johnston was to lead their group. If he had to be exhorted by some ranter, it had as well be a proper Presbyterian.

Andrew certainly felt a kinship with the man's opening words: "My brothers and sisters, I must confess that, at first, I was unwilling to preside at this great gathering for fear that it might lead to excesses and give occasion for the enemies of true faith to point at improprieties." Well, if he had to exhort, he couldn't have chosen a more appropriate subject than avoiding excess, Andrew thought.

Their leader continued. "Let us set the Lord God before us and so realize His awful presence in this place that good may be done and God may be glorified. We are especially met to do homage to the Holy Spirit, whose convincing and converting power has been so strikingly manifested amongst us for these several months. Let us not resist Him."

The minister had barely finished speaking when a girl who could not have been yet twenty years old faced the group. She was not a pretty lass, but there was a shine about her that was most refreshing. In plain words, spoken in a clear voice, she told that she had found peace on the previous Sabbath evening and that she was happy in the Lord. "Come to Jesus," she concluded, almost as an afterthought.

The effect of her simple invitation was like an electric shock. People all around Andrew dropped to their knees. "Lord Jesus, have mercy on me, a sinner" and similar cries came from all directions. On every side, people exhorted those who were seeking salvation, others wept and prayed aloud for mercy, some praised God for salvation, some were singing, "He took me from a fearful pit, and from the miry clay, and on a rock He set my feet…"

Bridget stood with hands clasped, tears streaming down her face. Andrew tugged roughly at her arm. "Come on. I've seen enough." She startled as if waking, crossed herself jerkily, and turned to him. "Oh. Yes, enough. Oh, yes." She followed him as he fought his way through the throng.

Movement became easier as they neared the edge of the garden, but untangling the carriage was another matter. By the time they were moving, it was too late to accomplish anything at the market—if one had even been held in the midst of all this lunacy. Imagine canceling market day for a religious gathering. Andrew's disgust knew no bounds.

They were making their way slowly back southward, having veered considerably out of their way in an attempt to avoid traffic, when Andrew heard that blasted song again, "What's the News?" A group of young voices shouted out the question.

The answer came from their fellows on the other side of

the pavement. "Oh, tell them you've begun to pray, that's the news!"

They seemed to be boys from some factory or home or school, all under the leadership of a man in clerical garb. At the end of the song, they formed into a more orderly procession and began a new hymn:

> *Here we suffer grief and pain,*
> *Here we meet to part again,*
> *In heaven we'll part no more.*
> *Oh, that will be joyful,*
> *Joyful, joyful…*

The final *joyful* was cut off by their black-suited leader. "Boys, boys, that's fine singing, that is. But I'd ask ye to pass quietly here now." Those in the back were still singing, unable to hear him, so the portly man jumped up on a cart beside the pavement and held out his arms. "Boys! Boys, hear me. That's a fine testimony to the power of the Spirit burning in your hearts."

Several cries of "Praise Jesus!" interrupted him.

"That's fine, but I'd have ye quieten now. Ye'll be noting we're approaching Durham Street, and I'm fearing our singing might be of disturbance to our Catholic neighbors. I ask you to desist. Let us bear silent witness to the love and courtesy our Savior asks us to show to one another as Christians."

The boys nodded assent, and the minister jumped down and set forth with a wave of his hand. "I'll give the signal when ye can start again, lads, when we're in the Shankill. We are not to provoke one another to wrath."

Andrew was soon able to turn eastward, but what he had just witnessed impressed him more than all the prayers, songs, exhortations, and phenomena he had heard or seen. Upwards of forty boys marched toward the Falls in a quiet, mannerly order, many with radiant smiles on their faces, and not a hint of a song or slogan that might be deemed provocative to that solidly Catholic neighborhood through which they passed.

So could there be something beyond emotion to this business of being stricken by the Spirit? He laughed and whipped up his team. Only two weeks until the Glorious Twelfth. Then they would see.

CHAPTER FOURTEEN

This year promised to be something special in the way of Orange marches. It was an anniversary year—the tenth anniversary of Dolly's Brae, when thirteen hundred Orangemen from around Castlewellan had chosen to march through an exclusively Catholic neighborhood with drums, songs, and loaded rifles. They had been met by a thousand Catholic Ribbonmen armed with pitchforks, pikes, and muskets.

No one ever knew who fired the first shot, but at the end of the day, the thirty or more corpses lying in the road were all wearing green ribbons.

Then, only two years ago, intense sectarian rioting had raged for ten days in the very area of working-class Belfast through which those revival boys had walked in silence.

So, they would see, indeed. Andrew allowed his mind to muse as he set out Grandfather Lanark's orange sash for Mrs. B to press. This year his lodge would support their brothers in County Antrim by joining the march from Ballymena to Toome. It promised to be as fine a gathering as any that celebrated the glorious anniversary of King Billy's victory. Finer than most, since the Ahoghill Old Fair was to be held nearby with liquor flowing freely to wet a man's throat after miles of dusty singing, and plenty of good card games and rousing cockfights for lively entertainment after the march.

Andrew couldn't remember ever having looked forward to a Glorious Twelfth more than he did this year. Now he understood the pleasure Grandfather Lanark used to take in such doings. He was certainly in the mood for a rousing march. A good loud band and a few rounds of singing "Ye Loyalists of Ireland" was just what he needed to shake off the depression he had been in for weeks.

The prayer meeting Tammis and Selma had invited him to had apparently borne fruit in Newtownards and Comber. Reports circulated of nightly prayer meetings that were attended by upwards of two hundred people all around the district. Andrew himself had even seen people kneel down in the Newtownards marketplace. Whenever there was a meeting announced, people dropped their other activities and went—anytime or anyplace. Even on Scrabo. Andrew grimaced at the thought of the open-air meetings being held almost in his backyard.

But that was better that than those in town, where weavers stopped their looms at the sound of singing and women dropped their muslin or went off to join the audience with their hoops in their hands.

Well, they had their revival. And much good it might do them. What any of them would do when the linen industry collapsed, Andrew couldn't imagine. And all for a lot of psalm singing.

Still, he had to admit that the revival songs had more life to them than the metricals. If there was any long-lasting result of all this brouhaha that he could approve of, it would be the newly installed organ in the Presbyterian Church. No sense letting the Methodists have all the good songs. But an Orange band and a good pounding of Lambeg drums could beat any organ he ever heard, and Andrew had never been in a finer mood to raise his voice. He would sing loud enough for himself and for his grandfather.

Andrew's exuberant, belligerent mood continued the next day.

Remember your allegiance,
Be this your Battle Cry,
For Protestant Ascendancy
In church and State we'll die!

He sang at the top of his voice as he drove Fairling at a brisk trot northward.

Ye Loyalists of Ireland,
Come, rally round the throne!

He had started through the ballad again when he began to wonder if he had his directions wrong. The lodge master had been very clear about the matter. They were to meet at Broughshane to form for the march. But as he drew near, something seemed amiss. He heard no booming of drums calling all loyal marchers to order, though the area seemed lively enough. Indeed, there were people everywhere, including the usual clutter of children and chickens that lined every march route.

He was almost there before he heard a boom. And it was not the cadence of a Lambeg drum. It was the booming voice of a man addressing a large crowd all sporting vibrant orange sashes.

Andrew couldn't understand how he could have arrived late. He hurried forward, not wishing to miss the Loyalist Charge or any last-minute instructions.

"And so, I can tell you that all are knit together in one holy band of Christian fellowship. The Presbyterian not annoying the Episcopalian, the Episcopalian not vexing the Presbyterian. I thank God that, in every convert I have spoken to, all their sectarianism fled and their love to the human family was such that if they could gather all their

Roman Catholic neighbors in their arms and carry them up to the third heaven, they would do so."

Andrew frowned. This was the strangest Loyalist Charge he had ever heard. He stood apart from the group and listened.

"I tell you, gentlemen, this brotherly love is a hallmark of the revival. I would say, even, that it is the hallmark. Neighbors once at variance now embrace each other. Animosities have passed away. Where there has been enmity, now there is love. Where there was revenge, now there is forgiveness…"

Jay Lanark's orange sash rested heavy around Andrew's shoulders as if it had stones attached to the ends. He had come to march for the power and industry that had made Ulster prosper, for the traditions his grandfather had lived for, for the values and lifestyle he held to and sweated for every day. He had not come for a revivalist rant.

Andrew turned on his heel and returned to his carriage. If they wanted to march for prayer and sermonizing, let them. If they wanted to sing psalms instead of Loyalist ballads, let them. He'd have no part of it. He knew where the real action would be anyway. Why wait until after the march? He'd get an early start. A good cockfight could take a man's mind off anything, and people came from miles around to the sport at Crae Rocks.

He wasn't disappointed. A rowdy crowd was gathered about the ring, cheering. Andrew put his money on a long-tailed Rochester Red to beat a scrappy-looking Wendham Gray. Men around Andrew punched the air with both fists as the Red attacked viciously, but the Gray was a stayer. The mob broke forth with cheers and raucous calls as the Red drew blood three times. Finally, the Wendham stumbled and Rochester could move in for the kill. Andrew, who had been leaning over the pit in his enthusiasm, drew back to wipe the sweat from his brow and discovered he was spattered with blood.

He wiped his palm on his handkerchief quickly before any should see. The stigmata phenomenon had been disproved. He wanted nothing to do with even the looks of any such thing.

The next pair of cocks were paraded around the ring by their owners.

And then a group of newcomers caught Andrew's attention. He stared. What were three parsons doing at a cockfight?

But the matter soon became clear. As Crae Rocks was annually the scene of carousing, cockfighting, and cardsharping, it seemed the revivalists had scheduled a service here. And looking beyond the cockpit, Andrew judged that nearly two thousand people had responded to their call. He turned back in disgust to place his money on Shaker's Blue as the newly-arrived enthusiasts began singing "What's the News?"

That song again. Andrew tried to shut it out and concentrate on the cockfight. He pulled his hat down and shook his head in a fruitless effort to avoid hearing the words.

For us He bowed His sacred head,
For us His precious blood was shed,
And now He's risen from the dead,

That's the News!

Andrew's cock was dragged from the pit, a mass of blood-soaked feathers, by the time the song ended. He turned to escape from the whole reddened area but could not shove a path through the throng that now tightened up the better to hear the preacher.

The parson announced his text. "Before the cock crows, thou shalt deny me thrice."

Andrew almost expected to hear an accompanying crow from the cockpit. The silence that followed was more chilling.

"Peter was in the same predicament as Paul later found himself when he wrote, 'For what I would, that do I not; but what I hate, that do I.' Perhaps some of you—nae, nae, all of us—all have found ourselves hating what we do, doing the very thing we said we would never do—"

Andrew nearly knocked the woman behind him to the ground in his effort to flee. What right did that preacher have to single him out? What did he know about what Andrew Armstrong did and did not want to do? How dare some prating parson accuse Andrew of hating what he did? He wanted to be like his grandfather. Of course, he did. He had decided of his own free will. No more the milksop of his former life; the man who let himself be trampled by events. Jay Lanark had been a fine man. He had stood up to everything and everybody. And Andrew had decided more than to be like him. He would *be* him.

What I would, that do I not; but what I hate, that do I. The words rang in his head until he would have thrust his hands over his ears had the crush of the crowd given him room.

He had just forced his way to the back when a young red-haired woman approached him with a smile. He would merely have brushed past her had she not looked so much like Bridget. As it was, he took the card she held out to him and jammed it into his pocket.

By the time Andrew reached Lanarks' Bawn, he wasn't sure whether he was hearing Lambeg drums, thunder, or the pounding of his own heart, but whatever it was, he had to exorcise the ghosts that compelled him. Perhaps that was it —who would have thought one could hear the feet of marching ghosts?

Was it only because it was the Glorious Twelfth that he felt driven by all those who had died in the '41, at Drogheda, at the Boyne, in the 1798 Rising, and in the Potato Famine? All those of *both* sides?

Andrew drew a sharp breath and looked around him. Where had such a question come from? The very audacity of it filled him with guilt. And yet with a strange buoyancy, too. Even as the thought formed, he felt the madness within him lessen its grip, he sensed a glimmer of hope breaking in. Was it possible?

The very fact that he could ask such a question must mean that Jay Lanark *hadn't* won after all. For Andrew's grandfather there had been no question of there being two sides to any matter. If Andrew could question the Orange position, he was not Jay Lanark. And if he wasn't Jay Lanark, Andrew Armstrong could ask his own questions and find his own answers. He could be himself—not driven to fulfill the demands of a ghost.

With the drumming still pounding in his head, he made his way to his study and took down the large, crumbling Bible from the highest shelf. The fact that he had to blow a cloud of dust from the cracked leather cover was further evidence of Mrs. B's waning vigor. And of Jay Lanark's absence. Grandfather had regularly taken down the volume to point out the name of every Lanark so carefully inscribed there: Calum who had built the Bawn. Dougal, his son who had fought with Cromwell. David and Graham, father and son who had fought at the Boyne…

But now Andrew focused on something Grandfather had never pointed out. Other names were there as well: Rory, who had married a Catholic and gone to live at Scaton Court. Isobel, who had married an O'Brien. Katrina, who had married Robert Price. And Aileen… That was the one who had run off with the MacHenry.

As his family tree lay spread out before him, it was as if

his own life branched and blossomed. It wasn't necessary to follow one narrow path to be true to his heritage. He wasn't predestined by birth to a course of action or of thought. That was exactly what he had once said himself—shouted even—when arguing with Grandfather.

He had tried to find purpose in carrying on the Lanarks' Bawn tradition—with all the rules and rigidity he had once rejected so vigorously. But one could not only reject. One must also accept—open oneself to meaning, to direction, to a higher power and purpose than oneself and one's own rules. One must embrace life and life's Creator.

Putting his hand in his pocket, he felt the card that girl had given him. It was headed "My Covenant." He read it through. Slowly. Three times.

I take God the Father to be my God.
I take Christ the Son to be my Savior.
I take the Holy Spirit to be my Sanctifier.
I take the Word of God to be my Rule.
I take the people of God to be my people.
I dedicate my whole self to the Lord.
And I do this deliberately,

and sincerely,

and freely,

and for ever.

He had just signed and dated the card when there was a light knock at the door.

"Come."

The threatening storm had rolled on, taking the dark clouds with it. Now the deep golden sunlight of a summer evening shone through the tall windows lining one side of the room. It fell on Bridget as she entered. The fact that Andrew was no longer consumed with hunger had nothing to do with the fine roast duck surrounded with potatoes that she was carrying.

Andrew took the platter from her and set it aside. Then he turned back to embrace Bridget and his new life.

CHAPTER FIFTEEN

1996

Mary dropped the manuscript onto the bed beside her and sat, dazed, for several moments. Finally, she turned her head to her bedside clock. How long had she been immersed in that story? It could have been a week, half a lifetime, or no time at all. It was as if she had become Andrew Armstrong and experienced the agony, the loss, the hunger, the bitterness, and the release herself. She knew the events were all from history, and yet she felt she could have experienced them in another universe.

Gradually, her own room, her own time, came back into focus. She stretched, turned on the radio, and reached for her hairbrush. Her movements were stiff and jerky, as if she were in a dream, but she had to function. Her clock told her that she just had time to get to the CCC for play practice. She did hope it would go well this evening. It had to. In the almost two weeks since they had begun again on the project they had made considerable progress, but not nearly enough. She would describe their successes as uneven at best.

At least Sheila's posters were brilliant. And the young people had distributed them all over Belfast. Which would be great if their production was good. If it wasn't, it would just mean that many more people would watch them fall on their faces.

She gave a final, swift glance to her image in the mirror: slim-fitting jeans, long-sleeved white shirt over a navy blue turtleneck, sleek golden hair. She slung her brown leather bag over her shoulder and reached to shut off the radio, then paused as the announcer's voice caught her attention.

"As the twelfth of August nears, tensions mount over planned marches in Londonderry and Belfast. Authorities say they fear the Apprentice Boys' marches may produce an even more violent confrontation than the sectarian violence that erupted over July's traditional Glorious Twelfth marches. Spokesmen from both communities—"

Mary snapped the speaker off mid-sentence. She had enough to worry about. She was glad that the church was holding special prayer meetings, and she knew that other congregations were doing the same. She just wished she had more faith. No matter how hard she tried, she couldn't shake the feeling that the whole country was on a giant treadmill, destined to repeat the same rounds of violence over and over.

On the M1 to Belfast, Mary shifted Sheila's little car to a higher gear, but she couldn't shift her mind out of its depression. Were she and Gareth on a giant treadmill, too? She envisioned each of them running round and round in interlocking wheels. At the moments those wheels touched, their love flared a sure, bright flame. But the eternal turning of the days kept flinging them apart so that they made no progress. Sometimes it seemed each turning pulled them further apart.

One of the things she loved most about Gareth was his compassion—his deep caring about these people, his work for them and the future of this country. And all seemingly undimmed by ending up in a walking cast from trying the defend the center from intruders in the middle of the night. She suppressed a sigh with gritted teeth. She tried, she really tried, to be as selfless as he was.

At the CCC she braked and shifted down to make the turn into her parking space.

Inside, she was met by a buzz of activity. This was to be their last rehearsal at the Centre. Next week they would begin rehearsals at Noah's Ark, where the actual performance would be. That cheering thought gave her a sense of progress.

A CD player lilted out a lively Irish melody while Fiona directed a line of step dancers. Mary smiled, noting how quickly her sisters Becca and Julie had caught the basic technique, even if they weren't as light on their feet as Fiona. Debbie appeared to be a natural. Her long, slim, shorts-clad legs moved effortlessly, and her dangling silver earrings swung in rhythm. It looked as though the Irish step-dancing was one part of "A Night in Olde Belfast" that Mary didn't have to worry about.

Sheila hurried across the room, her countenance shining like the gold silk blouse she wore. "Good news! We've just had a reply from the Development Council. They are terrifically interested in what you're doing. They're sending a whole delegation to the program. If we pull this off, it means we're almost assured funding for the youth center."

"Oh, that's great!" Mary tried to match her excitement and put out of her mind the niggling fear that said, *Yes, but if you fizzle, that'll tear the whole thing.*

She approached the dancers, clapping her hands. "Super! You're doing a great job. And I've got some really great news." She looked around. "But where are the rest of our musicians? I want to tell everyone at once."

Where were the musicians? Why were the dancers using recorded music? The musicians needed more practice than anyone else. She didn't worry much about Liam and Martin, who she spotted sitting in a corner with their instruments, looking bored, but Tommy had missed many practices lately, and Lila's harp was really what held the whole thing together.

As if they had heard her question, Lila came running down the concrete stairway that led from the upper offices. Tommy followed her, one hand gripping the banister, the other held out in a pleading gesture. Neither carried instruments. When Lila reached the lounge, Mary could see that her eyes were red and puffy.

Tommy came directly to Mary. "You tell her. Tell her it's not about me—it's for the kids."

Lila shook her head, tears still glimmering on her dark lashes. She turned back to Tommy with both hands out. "I've told you and told you—it's not me you have to convince. It's my parents. They're afraid—"

Tommy put his hands on her shoulders. "Lila, you're twenty-one years old. You're old enough to decide whether you play your clarsach in a program or not."

She shivered. "But Da says the IRA might…" She swallowed. "They might disrupt the whole show!"

"And your parents think I'm working with the Army." He turned his back to her, his hands gripping both sides of his head.

"No, they don't—" she started, then stopped. "Well, the police said—"

Liam rose from the floor where he'd been sitting, idly strumming a few chords. "There it is, man. See, it doesn't matter what you do—you'll get blamed for it anyway. It's better to act."

"Liam," Mary's voice reflected the dismay she felt. "You promised."

He shrugged. "Said I'd do the show. Didn't say what I'll do aftcr."

The show. That brought Mary back to her job. "Wait, everybody. I've got good news. Please. If we can just work together for a few more days. Just till the middle of

August." She sensed Lila edging toward the door. "Please. Just for tonight. If we can have a really good rehearsal tonight, then maybe we can work something out." She turned toward Lila. "Please, we really need you."

By a combination of Mary's cajolery and Sheila's good news the moment was rescued, and the rehearsal went on. They finished the musical numbers and were just beginning the play when the outside door opened, and Philip and Paddy O'Reilly walked through to Philip's office. Mary hoped the serious look on their faces wasn't a harbinger of more bad news.

She turned back to the action in the Bruin cottage. The characters lacked the magical lyricism Yeats' poetry required for the play to be a success—but at least, they all seemed to know their lines. That was a major hurdle crossed.

Liam fell to his knees, mourning Maire's death, and for an instant Mary felt her throat tighten. Yes, the magic was there—mostly too far below the surface to be seen—but it was there. If only she could bring it out.

Behind her, the office door opened. Paddy came out first. Mary's spirits rose. The old twinkle was back in his eyes and a broad smile on his ruddy face. "Well, there's good news and bad news and good news. But what did you expect? This is Ireland. First bit of good news is that Philip has been invited to speak at the peace rally in Dublin this weekend."

That announcement was greeted with enthusiasm. But then an uneasy quiet settled over the room. He had said bad news too.

"I won't mess you about. The bad news is that plans for cross-border cooperation programs have bogged down." Such announcements were so normal that reactions amounted to shrugs and raised eyebrows. "The one for a youth camp is the one I feel worst about. I'd worked hardest on that, and we had a good program set up—one that some of you boys and girls would maybe have liked to join. That's why I'm appealing for your help now."

Warning flags went up in Mary's head. They didn't need another failing project to rescue. They had more on their plate than they could begin to handle now. "Can it wait until after the show, Paddy? We've got those people from the council coming—"

"Aye, that's why we need to do this now. It'll clinch the leisure center sure if I can tell them how your young people banded together to work cross-border as well as cross-community."

"Paddy, there isn't time—"

He wasn't listening. "All I need is the leaders from each side of the street." He looked at Debbie and Liam. "Just a quick trip to Dublin. I've got it all set up. And since Philip says he needs to meet his URU people in Enniskillen anyway—"

Paddy bounded on, explaining, while Mary groped for a chair. She needed to see a map to be certain, but she was pretty sure Dublin was anything but on the way to Enniskillen. This would require at least two, probably three, days away. Right when they were in such a critical time crunch.

"Oh, can we go to the peace rally, too?" Becca never missed anything.

"Dublin! Cool!" Julie was always right behind her.

"Gareth and Liam can bring their guitars. Imagine singing 'Bind Us Together' at a peace rally!"

The twins seemed to have taken over the peace rally plans. The next thing Mary knew, they would be getting up an Irish/American exchange and putting her in charge of it.

In the end, Mary didn't really have any arguments that could stand up to Paddy and her energetic sisters. So, the next day, the same group that had journeyed to the west now crowded into the blue minibus and joined Paddy's expedition south. Mary wasn't quite certain how it had all come about, and she didn't know why Tommy was there, but she suspected it might have been a compassionate move on Philip's part to get him away from his girlfriend troubles.

Oh, well. Things were out of her control. She might as well enjoy herself. She'd tucked Philip's final manuscript in her bag. If nothing else, she might have time to get some reading done while the others were in meetings.

She was really pleased to be getting to see Dublin. Besides, she could always hope that the scheme might result in some time alone with Gareth. She looked at him, sitting next to her on the seat but a hundred miles away mentally.

He looked back with a sigh. "I wish I could think of something."

"Something for what?"

"The Ulster Reconciliation Union meeting in Enniskillen."

"The one you missed last time."

"That's right. They want to promote a nonpolitical, really grassroots program—something that will make a change inside people—where, of course, it all has to start. But no one has been able to come up with a fresh idea."

Mary laughed. "Sounds like they're looking for a revival." Then she paused. "Seriously, I just read about an amazing one here in 1859."

Gareth nodded. "Yes—but again, that was mostly only on one side of the road. Anything that doesn't reach all the people won't work."

"What about this peace rally?"

"Oh, aye. A fine thing. But it doesn't go deep enough. We need something more. A peace rally is fine for letting people express their thoughts and hopes, but it doesn't really change anyone's heart."

Mary wished with all her heart that she had something to offer. They passed the enormous security installations on the border at Newry. She could sense Liam tense as they stopped at the checkpoint, as if he were already IRA and feared inspection. Then they headed straight south toward Drogheda.

She considered the troubled lives in their one small vehicle. How much of that was a legacy of "the curse of

Cromwell"? Fortunately, no one else seemed to be thinking of that particularly gloomy subject.

Philip did, however, take a westward turning off the motorway. "We'll just take a little jaunt up here, since I know Mary's interested in history."

It wasn't Cromwell he had in mind. "King Billy's Glen," Philip said. They drove up a beautiful meadow where a smooth, swift-flowing river ran a silver ribbon through the deep emerald. He pointed out the knoll to the northwest where King James' troops had massed. Today the only activity was two little black waterhens that scurried through thick brush to their nests alongside the river.

Philip and Paddy were at their usual jovial bickering over the long-term results of the Battle of the Boyne, but Mary concentrated on the scenery. The glen was grown solid. Ivy and moss clung to oak and elm. Sheep grazed in the meadow beyond. She had seldom seen a more secluded, peaceful scene. There was no interpretative display, no visitors' center, no audiovisual presentation. Just green grass, silver water, and cream-colored sheep. And a large green and orange sign with flags fluttering atop, proclaiming "Boyne Battlefield Crossing, 1690."

"There was a stone obelisk down by the river at the place King Billy crossed. But the IRA blew it up in 1922." Philip offered the information without comment.

A few minutes later the Boyne was behind them, and Paddy was pointing out the window to a tall, bare mountain streaking by. "Ah, and there now's the Hill of Slane.

And isn't it a grand sight? The very spot where St. Patrick lit the Pascal Fire on Easter Eve."

"Oh." Mary hoped it was a reasonably intelligent sounding *oh*.

"And just down here—" they whipped around a corner and turned onto a southbound road, "you'll see Tara in just a minute."

"Okay."

"Ah, there. The green hill through the trees."

Well, everything was green through the trees. But one mound did seem taller than the rest.

"Home of the High Kings of Ireland for centuries. And doesn't the very name conjure up images of the glories of a civilization long silenced? It was from here that King Lóegaire saw Patrick's flame on Slane. The High King had Patrick brought to him in chains, because the king had forbidden anyone to light a fire that night. But when the druids saw Saint Patrick's fire, they said it was a flame that could never be extinguished. Lóegaire gave Patrick permission to preach Christianity in Ireland—so it's seeming the druids knew what they were talking about.

"There's not a lot to see there now—not with the physical eye, you understand. But for those of us with an eye for the spiritual—ah, well… And there's the Lia Fáil still standing in the center of it all."

"Oh! The Lia Fáil!" Now he had Mary's attention. She smiled as Paddy waxed eloquent over the ancient Stone of Destiny, which cried out its approval at the inauguration of a true High King. She reached across the seat and gave

Gareth's hand a squeeze. They had spent a whole summer tracking the Stone of Scone, which some believed to have come from the Lia Fáil, and she well knew that particular piece of Irish history.

Paddy barely had time to catch his breath before he pointed out the other side. "And there's Newgrange." And since Paddy never needed much time to catch his breath, he went on, telling her about the stone age grave—older than the pyramids.

Well, it was interesting. And she appreciated his pointing out the sights, when he would probably have rather been talking strategy with Philip. She had started her summer anxious to learn all she could of Irish history. But now she was feeling just a bit overdosed—especially as the more she learned of history here, the more she understood how deep the problems around her today were.

Mary suddenly felt she would rather simply focus on the present—even if it led only to shallow, short-term solutions. Right now, she would settle for any solution that would just last long enough for Gareth and her to get back across the Irish Sea to Scotland. She gave his hand a final squeeze.

They crested a small hill, and Paddy threw out his hands. "Ah, and isn't that a sight to gladden the heart of any true Irishman—even one from occupied Ireland?" It was a sign of the depth of their friendship that Philip smiled in assent as Paddy continued. "'Dublin's fair city'— Dubh Linn. That's meaning the Dark Pool to those without the gift of the Gaelic. And running right through the middle, the River Liffey—the River of Life." Paddy glanced at his watch. "Ah, fine. Ye did a brisk job of the driving, Philip. We'll just have time for a wee ride about before our meeting."

Philip raised an eyebrow. "That Irish time, Paddy? You know how I feel about being late to meetings."

Paddy laughed. "Ah, if it's Irish time you're on, we'll have time for a meal." He turned to Mary. "You know what they say: the Irish have just one meal a day—all day." Then back to Philip. "That's it, just turn down O'Connell Street here. The colleen will be wanting to have a wee peek at the GPO."

Philip shook his head. "Only in Dublin would the General Post Office be the first place you'd take a tourist."

It was, however, a magnificent building with an impressive portico lined with enormous Ionic columns.

"The scene of the 1916 Rising," Paddy said in the same tone of voice he might have used concerning an ancient church. "It was the main stronghold of the volunteers fighting for independence." He pointed to the middle of the street. "Ah, and we'll just take a wee peek at the Parnell monument."

"You'll be spending all day showing her statues of your troublemakers, Paddy." But Philip paused as requested before a fine stone column topped by a bronze flame. At the base was the statue of the powerful member of Parliament who led the fight for Irish Home Rule in the late nineteenth century—until a scandal with a colleague's wife brought his downfall.

At the next embellishment to Dublin's main thoroughfare, however, Paddy did not suggest they stop. He merely waved a freckled hand at a fountain splashing forth water over the head of a marble female. "Aye, a bit of local art more popularly known as *The Floozie in the Jacuzzi.*

"And the Abbey Theatre is just a block up there."

"Oh!" Now he had Mary's full attention. How she would love to see "The Playboy of the Western World" or "Juno and the Paycock" at the very theater that gave them birth.

At the foot of the street, Paddy pointed out further statues, but Becca had a low tolerance for historical sights. "Where's *Molly Malone?*"

"Aren't there any shops?" Julie seconded her sister's restlessness.

"Just you wait. Along here in a minute—some of the best shopping in the world." Paddy O'Reilly wasn't given to understatement.

Across O'Connell bridge, bustling Grafton Street's tangle of colorful shops and pubs were crowded with patrons being serenaded by street musicians, all watched over by a life-sized bronze statue of *Sweet Molly Malone* pushing her wheelbarrow of cockles and mussels and calling, "Alive, alive-o."

"Now, we'll let you out right here," Philip said. "*Sweet Molly* makes a good meeting place. Say in two or two and a half hours." He pulled a map of the city from the glove box and handed it to Mary. "You're centrally located here."

She found Grafton Street, then followed his finger to

the west. "Right here at Christ Church Cathedral is Dublina, a reconstruction of life in medieval Dublin. Twins might enjoy that if they get tired of shopping."

"Or run out of money—which is more likely." Mary winked at her sisters.

"Back over here—" he pointed to the east of Grafton Street, "is the National Museum. Some of the finest Early Christian art in existence: Saint Patrick's Bell, the Tara Brooch, Viking relics…"

Mary could see her sisters' eyes glazing over. "That's all right, Philip. Thanks."

"Ah, but for my money, the Book of Kells is the best thing in Dublin," Paddy spoke up.

"Oh, yes. I'd love to see that!"

Philip pointed to Trinity College on the map. "Right there. Easy walking distance. But you may have to queue. Very popular exhibit." Mary's face fell. She would gladly stand in line for as long as it took to see the world's most beautiful book. But there was little chance she could talk Becca and Julie into the idea.

Tommy must have seen her disappointment. "I'm not really needed at your meeting, am I, Philip?" he said. "I could show the girls around. Leave Mary free to see what she wants."

Philip not only agreed but, even better, suggested that Gareth join Mary, since his main purpose in coming was to attend the Enniskillen meeting tomorrow. So, she watched her sisters happily trip off with their escort in search of fish and chips.

Mary and Gareth walked along the crowded sidewalk hand in hand, barely hampered by his cast. To their left was the Ionic-columned Bank of Ireland, built in the eighteenth century to house the Irish Parliament. Across the street, they turned toward the Corinthian portico of Trinity College.

But in jarring contrast to the classical architecture, here they were confronted with reminders of the turmoil on this small island. A black and white sign strapped to a lamppost blared: "Dublin's prisoners—Britain's hostages."

Mary wasn't even sure she understood what they were saying, but the sentiment was the same as that which moved the rebels to the action that leveled O'Connell Street nearly a hundred years ago. She breathed much easier when the next three lampposts held announcements of the peace rally to be held that evening in Phoenix Park.

Then they entered the wide quadrangle of Trinity College.

"Oh, my." Mary looked at the queue snaking past the buildings that surrounded the grassy square. But she really didn't mind. It was a beautiful day, and she was sharing it with the man she loved. It was good just to be standing there chatting about nothing much in particular. Just being together.

They talked about their hopes for the success of the peace rally—especially that it would get good media coverage. Then Gareth told her a little of what he hoped to accomplish at tomorrow's meeting. She smiled and agreed.

But at that moment she felt she would have smiled and agreed to anything he chose to say.

And then they were at the library.

Mary was disappointed to learn that the famous Book of Kells wasn't actually made by Saint Columba's own hand. It was probably done by monks from Iona when Viking attacks drove them to Kells in the year 807.

But there was no disappointment when she walked around the well-lighted glass case containing the actual book. The ancient tome had been rebound with each gospel in a separate volume so that more could be displayed at one time. The pages were turned weekly. Mary tried to calculate how long it would take a person to see the entire work at that rate, but she abandoned calculations to lose herself in the detailed beauty of the page displayed before her.

Even after they left the college and sat in a quiet shop over afternoon tea, she couldn't quit thinking about the beauty of the work she had seen and the endless hours of devotion that had been poured out by countless monks working in the most primitive of conditions. The overwhelming thing was not the time involved, the infinite attention to detail, or even the rich creativity, but rather the love for the Word of God that the production of such a treasure exemplified.

And then they had to hurry back to *Molly Malone* to meet their group.

Spirits were high in the minibus. Debbie and Liam had apparently impressed the committee with their enthusiastic talk about their youth councils and how they were working together to build a leisure center. Apparently, Liam had kept his sympathies for the IRA well hidden. She could hope he had even had a change of heart. Debbie was glowing about what a fine idea she thought the exchange program was. She would love to spend a summer living in Dublin.

She was even more enthusiastic when Philip turned into Phoenix Park. "Oh, this is beautiful! What a great flower garden. My mum would love it."

Paddy explained with the considerable pride of a born Dubliner that this was the largest enclosed public park in Europe. And there was the residence of the president of the Republic of Ireland. "And the American ambassador's residence. Now, isn't that a fine sight to be standing side by side?" He turned in his seat with a wink for Mary.

By now the traffic was increasing enough that even Philip was forced to slow down. A green double-decker bus draped with white ribbons lumbered in front of them, bringing people from downtown to the park. Philip found a parking spot, and they joined the crowd funneling toward a high, white cross. Somehow that made the spot seem perfect for a peace rally. What better symbol of peace and unity?

A smiling, red-haired young mother with a fat baby in a pram and three young children smiled at Mary. The little girl closest to her held out a white ribbon.

"Oh, thank you!" Then she saw that workers everywhere were handing out ribbons. She was delighted to be part of the intent throng, all wearing white ribbons and waving homemade peace posters: "Give Us Back Our Peace," "Ceasefire," "No More Bombs." It was particularly poignant that so many of the signs had apparently been made by children. And it was important that this was in the south. A vast majority of these people would be avid Nationalists, like Paddy. But they did not support the violence that had torn their island apart for thirty years.

The CCC delegation edged as close to the speaker's platform as they could, and Mary looked around, wondering how many people were there. Thousands, surely. As far as she could see there were hopeful faces, white ribbons, waving posters.

A beautiful black-haired girl went to the microphone and sang "Lord, Make Me an Instrument of Thy Peace." The response following her song was warm and encouraging, but there was a seriousness to the occasion that kept down any of the elation usually shown at a concert. The mood was neither jubilant, nor militant, as Mary had rather expected it to be. She almost had the feeling of being in church.

The event was thoroughly ecumenical. Father Eamonn, a Catholic priest, prayed for the victims of violence and that God would grant political leaders on both sides of the divide "the serenity to accept the things they cannot change, the courage to change the things they can, and the wisdom to know the difference." Many in the crowd responded with fervent amens or crossed themselves.

A Presbyterian pastor spoke, followed by a Methodist

minister, then a Church of Ireland archdeacon, all expressing the deep desire of their people for peace. And then Philip took the stand, and Mary pressed farther forward.

"There is good news!" His proclamation was met with smiling, though reserved, anticipation.

"The peace we all seek is possible. But we must seek it at the right source. Not in politics, not in arms, but in the One who has called us to live in peace. There will be a political settlement—soon, we hope. But there have been political settlements before. None have lasted. Lasting peace won't be just a political settlement. Lasting peace must start with each one of us. The Prince of Peace will give us peace within ourselves to give to others and to spread over our land.

"When there is peace in the heart, there will be peace in the home. When there is peace in the home, there will be peace in the nation. Pray for the peace of Ireland. But first, pray for God's peace within your own heart."

He turned to Gareth and Liam, who stood on the platform with him, carrying their guitars. They began the song that had become the theme of so many gatherings, "Bind us together, Lord. Bind us together with cords that cannot be broken…"

Most of the crowd seemed to know the song, and those who didn't picked it up quickly. "Bind us together with love."

They were on the second time through when people began taking one another's hands. "There is only one God, there is only one King…" And then, with hands locked, people raised their arms, swaying in rhythm with the song. "Bind us together with cords that cannot be broken."

The rally ended with a full minute of silence. All across the largest park in Europe, thousands of people bowed, seeking the love that would bind them together.

At every exit, workers offered pages of the peace book for any who wished to sign a petition urging all leaders and people to work for peace. Mary wholeheartedly wanted to sign. Her one signature wouldn't make any difference to Irish leaders. But it made a difference to her. It was a concrete act, putting her name on the line. It would make her feel more a part of these people. But she didn't know about the proprieties. Perhaps one had to be a registered voter.

She approached the table. "Is it all right for an American to sign?"

"Oh, and is it your first trip to Ireland?" A ruddy-faced man smiled at her.

Mary said that, indeed, it was her first visit.

"Well, may it never be your last!" He held out a pen, and Mary thought of the irony that the Irish were the most welcoming, accepting people in the world—to everyone but each other.

CHAPTER SIXTEEN

They were perhaps an hour out of Dublin the next morning when Philip stopped in the center of a small town. "And would you like to take a wee peek at what's left of Saint Columcille's monastery?"

"You mean we're in Kells?" Mary had read about the monastery yesterday at the exhibit, but she'd had no idea they would be driving through the town.

"That's right. Thought you'd like to see where the famous book was made."

"Oh, yes, thank you." She bounded out of the vehicle and hurried up the narrow street.

Kells had been raided four times by Vikings after the monks had fled there to escape Norse raids on Iona. But in the warm gold of an Irish summer morning it was easy to recapture the peace of the place that had given the world *The Book of Kells*.

Mary was fascinated by St. Columcille's House, which

was really a tiny church. A plaque said that Columba had founded the monastery around the year 550, before he established work on Iona. And monks who returned here from Iona two hundred fifty years later produced the famous book—bringing history full circle. Dark green firs bordered the churchyard, and invisible birds sang from their boughs, just as they must have hundreds of years ago.

As the visitors returned to the minibus, Mary couldn't shake the feeling that had been pushing at her and growing in intensity ever since she'd seen *The Book of Kells*. It had been increased by the devotional atmosphere of the peace rally yesterday. She ran a finger over the white peace ribbon she still wore pinned to her lapel.

A gentle floating mist bathed the countryside as they continued their trek northward across rolling farmland. Mary sat in contemplation beside Gareth, trying to find a focus for the thoughts chasing around in her head: Kells, the monastery and the book, the timelessness and power of the Word of God, the contribution of His ministers who had achieved things of lasting value, the longing of the people expressed at the rally yesterday...

It was odd, the change the past twenty-four hours had made in her feelings. Now she agreed with Gareth—everything they had been working on was too shallow. A cross-border exchange, "A Night in Olde Belfast," even if they had dozens of peace rallies, something more was needed. All the things they had been working on were good things. But they were so... so... well, for want of a better word, they were so secular.

Maybe self-centered was a better word. They were working for themselves, for each other to some extent, but they needed a higher purpose. Art, music, folklore, and history all were part of what made Ireland special, but these would not make a lasting difference. The more she thought, the more uneasy she became. Had she missed something fundamental in her whole summer of work?

As they crossed the border back into Northern Ireland, she turned to Gareth and tried to express her troubling, confused thoughts.

He listened, then nodded. "I know. I keep trying to define our goals. I don't mean just the youth center or the production but the meaning behind them." He was quiet for a moment, then turned in his seat to look squarely at her. "What do you really want, Mary?"

She thought for a moment. "Well, I guess the same thing everybody in Ireland wants—peace and unity. You know—'Bind us together.'"

"Right—" He was obviously waiting for her to continue.

"But singing about it isn't enough. There's something else we must do. And I don't have a clue what it is. I feel so useless."

Gareth pulled out a note pad. "I didn't sleep much last night—had this afternoon's meeting on my mind. I got to thinking about one of the theologians we studied at university. Maurice was his name. He believed that the unity of mankind can be expressed only in worship, because that is where we make our common acknowledgment that God is our heavenly Father and that we are therefore brothers."

She nodded. "That makes sense. We sort of had that feeling at the rally when everyone held hands and sang."

"And Maurice believed that this unity could best be experienced at the one part of worship that is the Christian's highest privilege, the supreme moment in worship that is a reenactment of Christ's sacrifice for all mankind…" He paused as if waiting for her to supply the word.

"Communion." She said it slowly. "Yes." Then she frowned. "So? Christians take the sacraments all the time."

"In their own churches. In their own way. But not together."

"Together? You mean believing Catholics and Protestants? In the same service?" The concept was breathtaking. "I don't think that could be done. Catholics have very strict rules about that. My cousin married a Catholic. He couldn't even receive Communion at his own wedding. Really upset my aunt."

Gareth sat back. "Yep. But if there were some way it could be done, just think how powerful that could be." He leaned forward to the front seat and repeated his thoughts to Philip and Paddy.

Both were intrigued, but neither had a solution. "Interfaith rallies, prayer meetings, and song services are done rather often," Philip said.

"The BBC did an interfaith thing near us a few years ago. 'Songs of Praise.' My mum was involved," Debbie said from the backseat.

"Was she, now?" Paddy asked. "I was there myself. Fine singing that night, even with the C of I. Everyone knows the Methodists can sing. But this idea of Eucharist together… now that's a different matter."

"That's what makes the idea so special," Mary insisted. "The most sacred moment in all Christian worship through the ages—for all believers to put all differences aside and gather around the Lord's table…"

But no one could see how it could be done.

It was midafternoon when they drove across the bridge, through yet more security barricades, and into Enniskillen. Philip stopped in front of the hotel. "Hope they have room for us."

"Shall I go ask?" Mary slid her door open. "Two rooms enough? Boys and girls?"

As soon as she opened the hotel door, she heard music coming from the back. Probably the bar. The lounge television was also booming. There were people everywhere. A young man in a side room raised his glass and called a salute to someone in the lobby. A group of gray-haired women sat trying to hold a conversation over the blare of the television. A little girl in a flowered dress and shiny patent shoes skipped down the stairs beyond the desk. She was followed by a pair of little boys in white shirts and short dark pants.

Mary picked her way through the crowd to the woman

at the desk. "Do you have any rooms for tonight? We need two."

"Oh, Lord love you, dearie. We've aplenty. And don't you worry about all this. They'll quiet down. Not staying here, they aren't."

Mary smiled. "What is it? A wedding?"

"No, no, love. It's a funeral."

Mary blinked. "Oh." *How very Irish*, she thought, then turned back to business. She told the manageress what they would need. "But I can see you're busy. We've got some things to do, so we'll check in later."

The men had their meeting to attend. The twins spotted a pizza parlor. And Mary, who had been gripped on their last time through Enniskillen by Philip's account of the Remembrance Sunday massacre, wanted to get better acquainted with the town.

If one didn't know of the outrage that had occurred here, she thought, the casual passer-by would think this merely a more than usually tidy town square. The storefronts had been rebuilt, the war memorial replaced. She walked around, trying to imagine what the massacre must have been like. She had little success building the scene in her mind, although the threatening rain did provide a somber atmosphere.

After circling the square twice, Mary stopped at a newsagent's and found a book Philip had told her about. Then, as it was long past lunchtime, she found a quiet tea shop and opened the book while waiting for her scone. The cover showed a smiling young woman with warm brown eyes, wearing a nurse's cap.

It was tradition. Gordon Wilson and his daughter Marie always went to the wreath-laying ceremony at the war memorial cenotaph on Remembrance Day while Mrs. Wilson prepared Sunday dinner. The ceremony on November 8, 1987, was exactly like all the others—the band, the flag, officials to lay the wreath, all the town turned out to honor their war dead.

Until eleven o'clock.

A bomb exploded directly behind the Wilsons. A three-story building crashed down on them. There had been a moment of sinister silence, then shouting, moaning, screams of agony. Gordon and Marie Wilson lay buried beneath several feet of rubble.

"She held my hand tightly, and gripped me as hard as she could. She said, 'Daddy, I love you very much.' Those were her exact words to me, and those were the last words I ever heard her say."

Mary's tea cooled, untouched, as she read on. Eleven people had been killed. Sixty-three injured, nineteen of them severely. And that night Marie Wilson's father gave the BBC interview that rocked the world.

"I have lost my daughter, and we shall miss her. But I bear no ill will. I bear no grudge. She was a great wee lassie. She loved her profession. She was a pet. She's dead. She's in heaven, and we'll meet again. Don't ask me, please, for a purpose. I don't have an answer. But I know there has to be a plan. If I didn't think that, I would commit suicide. It's part of a greater plan, and God is good. And we shall meet again."

Reaction to the outrage came from President Reagan, Pope John Paul II, the Soviet news agency TASS, the lord mayor of Dublin, the rock group U2, and on and on. But none had the impact of those words from the quietly grieving father. Loyalist paramilitaries admitted a few days later that they were planning massive retaliation but were stopped by Wilson's words.

Mary turned to the family photos in the middle of the book, but her eyes were too blurred to see them properly. How could he do it? How could anyone have that much grace? As at the first time she heard the story, she asked herself what her response would be in such a situation. She hoped she would never have to find out.

Mary had spent far longer in the tea shop than she had thought possible. But it seemed the Reconciliation Union meeting had gone on overtime as well. She was hurrying toward the hotel when she saw the men approaching from the other direction.

As always, her eyes sought out Gareth first. He was so alive. Even after a long day, his eyes were shining. She linked her arm in his. "How did the meeting go?"

"Ah, it was brilliant. I told them what we'd been talking about. A priest there said he'd heard of something like that being done at Catholic/Protestant weddings. They call it an Agape Service."

Mary thought a moment. "Yes, I like the name."

"So did the Reconciliation Union people. They

appointed committees to work on it—everything. Now if I could just come up with a way to make it really nation-wide. This can't be a hole-in-the-corner event—not if it's to accomplish its potential."

Mary still wasn't convinced that anything could make the kind of difference he was looking for. But Gareth was so elated, she didn't want to be a wet blanket.

He talked on, explaining his hopes and ideas, then paused to make a note. "Ah, that's good. I want to remember that in the morning."

"What's in the morning?'

"We're having another meeting."

She groaned. "You're meeting again?" Why couldn't they get on with things? Why did everything have to be so slow? She felt as if she were caught in a time warp trap—and the more she knew about this place the more she felt that way. Reading that book today had brought it home to her again. Over and over and over again, the 1641 Rising, the 1987 Enniskillen massacre, events just kept repeating themselves. The merry-go-round would never stop. She wanted off.

"Mary, I know how you feel about this, but please be patient just a little longer. Getting everyone together around the Lord's Supper really could be the beginning of lasting peace. It's worth our total commitment." She wasn't going to take up that argument again. "I'm tired. Just show me to my room."

The request sounded simpler than it turned out to be, however. The wake continued full swing. The manageress was distracted four or five times before she actually led them up the stairs. And it was considerably later than that before she had them sorted out into workable rooms. The first she took the women to looked very pretty with its rose-covered comforters. But when Becca tossed her backpack on one of the beds, a leg collapsed, and it crashed to the floor.

"Well, now, that's no problem. The room next door is empty. You can just have it." So the manageress went back downstairs to get the keys, then went off to lead the men up another flight of stairs.

When Debbie turned down the cover on the bed she and Mary would share, the sheets were damp.

"Oh, I don't believe this." Mary started for the door.

"Wait." Julie stopped her. "The mattress pad is dry. Why not just pull the sheets off and sleep under the comforter?"

Mary was too tired and hungry to argue. It had been a very long day. She decided to give her hair a brush, then realized her bag was still in the mini. "Oh, Becca, toss me your brush."

"Yeah, here. Then let's go eat."

"Yes, hurry, I'm starved!"

"How about fish and chips?" At least her sisters were normal.

Mary finished with a quick flip of the brush and tossed it back to Becca. "I'll go ask if there's a chip shop somewhere close."

She met Tommy in the hall. One glance at his face stopped her. "What's wrong?"

"Ah, Mary, I'm sorry to tell you this."

"What?"

"I just called home. The show—the kids—they were working on the sets at Noah's Ark. Seems some kind of fight broke out. Frightened some of the daycare children. I'm not sure what happened, but Lila sounded pretty upset. Anyway, it's definitely off."

Mary put a hand over her face to hide her reaction. She should have been upset. After all the effort she had put into that program, this should be a blow. Instead, she found it blessedly liberating. Now she could leave. Now there was nothing she had to stay for. Except Gareth. And he could finish his work at that meeting in the morning. He could turn in his proposal, and they could leave. She closed her eyes and for a moment could hear the seagulls and feel the breeze on her face as they stood together on the ferry.

She hurried down the hall to find him. She was at the stairs when she met the men coming back down from above, carrying their luggage.

"Plumbing broken," Philip announced.

Mrs. McCarthy, still smiling and with her keys jangling, was unphased. Apparently this was a common occurrence.

Everyone trooped upward and found a room with working taps at the back of the fourth floor. At least the cold water worked. No one felt like asking for more. Except for directions to the chip shop.

Philip and Tommy started out, taking the key to turn in at the desk. But Gareth sat on a bed, still bent over his notepad.

"Oh, come on, Gareth. You can make your notes later. Everyone's starving." Mary's protest was none too patient. She wanted his attention so that she could tell him the good news—that their work here was done.

Gareth, however, seemed anything but finished. "You go on. I'm not very hungry. I want to work on this."

"Gareth, I have great admiration for your drive and devotion. But this is silly. You've done your part. You got the idea started. The committees can carry it on. They've done interfaith services before."

"That's the point. It isn't just another service. It's Communion."

"So?"

He took her hands and sat her on the edge of the bed next to his. "Mary, I guess I forget how new all this is to you. The Lord's Supper is a love feast that all believers are commanded to participate in—together. It's a memorial of His sacrifice on the cross."

"I know that."

He gripped her hands tighter, his eyes shining. "And in Communion we come to the table as members of His family—and we recognize each other as members. Members of Christ. Believers are one."

"That's great, Gareth, it really is. And I expect it will happen—someday. But can't you get it through your head that such reconciliation is not going to happen now?"

She clamped her mouth shut, trying not to sigh—or scream. She knew she needed to be calm and reasonable—no matter how unreasonable the world seemed at the moment. Why couldn't she get through to him that they had done all that was humanly possible here? They had done their best—and beyond. There was nothing more they could do. They were done. *Finis.*

She allowed herself a deep breath. "Look, Gareth, I spent all summer on that program. Tickets were selling well. The development council was coming. The kids knew their lines. There was nothing more anyone could have done. And now it's all off. Just like that. These people can't work together. They never have. They never will. Not even believers. So, you might as well come eat fish and chips with us."

She should have saved her breath to cool her chips.

It was as if he hadn't even heard her. Her declaration that it was all over hadn't even registered with him. "There's so much to do. And the time is so short."

Choking back her frustration, she fought to try to understand. He wasn't hearing her; she should at least try to hear him. "You mean you expect violence at the Londonderry marches?"

"Who knows? It may not wait that long."

"What do you mean?"

He jerked to his feet and began pacing in the little half-step way his walking cast required. "The peace process is too slow. Tempers are too short. That was true even before things bogged down over the marches. The word is that there's a power struggle within the leadership of the IRA. The peace faction there may not be able to keep control."

He returned to her side in two quick strides and took both her hands in his. "Mary, I do understand your impatience. You were so good to come here at all. And I know it hasn't been easy."

Easy? She bit her lip and turned away from him. It had been the hardest summer of her life. And she had accomplished nothing for all her effort. The sooner she got away from here the better.

"Please try to hold on a little longer." He dropped to his knees in front of her and reached out with both hands, taking hers between his, as if folded in prayer. "Mary, it isn't just that I need to make notes for my talk. What I really want—need—is to spend some time praying."

She made a sound of contempt, then was sorry when she saw how that reaction hurt him.

But he didn't back down. "We only have a window of time. A small window and it may be closing."

His words chilled her. And perhaps because she was frightened, she reacted in anger. She jerked her hands away and turned from him. "Good! Let it slam shut. It serves them right—the whole lot of them!"

"You don't mean that."

She turned back, her hands on either side of her head, as if to suppress a scream. "Gareth, I'm sorry. I know how much this means to you. But I'm not a sanctified saint. I can't accept this 'not my will but Thine' stuff. And I've had enough. I worked hard on that program. I was committed to it—and to those kids. But they can't even work together long enough to put on a music and drama show. It's just stupid, blind optimism to think they'll come together politically or religiously."

She strode to the door. "I've had it. I can't take any more." She jerked the door open. "I'm sorry, Gareth. I'm sorry." She pulled the ring from her finger and threw it behind her as she fled.

CHAPTER SEVENTEEN

In the glaring, overheated chip shop where she caught up with the others, Mary tried to push Gareth's words out of her mind. Most of their group were crowded into one large booth. Tommy and Liam, the last to receive their orders because they waited for a fresh frying of haddock, sat on the counter stools facing the window. She doused her steaming cod fillet in salt and malt vinegar, then closed her eyes so as to enjoy the first bite more fully. Crisp, golden batter; tender, juicy fish. There was nothing like it.

She really couldn't think about the scene with Gareth right now. One corner of her mind was screaming: *You broke up with Gareth. You threw his ring at him. You just ended everything you've dreamed of for three years.* But another part of her tried to argue that now she was free. Free of her commitments to him. Free of her commitments to Ireland. Free to leave and be her own person.

She tried to concentrate on the salty, vinegary taste of the fish. She was starving, and this was about the best fish she'd ever tasted. So why was it so hard to swallow?

A chrome stool clattered onto the linoleum floor, and her eyes snapped open. She dropped her fish back onto its bed of chips as Tommy flung open the door and darted up the street. Liam bolted after him, shouting obscenities.

It was several minutes before Tommy returned, shaking his head. "Lost him."

"What was that all about? Who were you chasing?" Philip demanded.

"Joe Navan."

"What? Are you sure?"

"Haven't seen him for five years, but I'm sure. That white-blond hair and protruding nose—who could miss it? I've even seen him carry packages just like that for the Army." Then Tommy seemed to realize what he'd said. "Oh, God!"

He had spoken the words as a prayer, but Mary was too shocked to pray. Tommy had chased an IRA member, carrying a package that could be a bomb—going in the direction of the hotel.

"Gareth!" She wasn't sure whether she had whispered or shouted. She only knew she was on her feet, running. Out of the corner of her eye she saw Philip dashing toward the phone box across the street.

Then all she saw was dark streets blurring past her and the look on Gareth's face when she threw the ring at him. All she felt was the hardness of the pavement as her feet slapped against it and the searing dryness in her throat as air rasped in forced gulps.

She had to get there in time. She had to warn Gareth. And the others. Pictures flashed before her eyes: a little girl in a party dress, singing as she skipped down the stairs; a group of grandmothers, gray heads bent together as they shared old memories; a young couple, laughing over a joke; a new mother sitting quietly in a corner nursing her baby…

And then the scene twisted in her mind. The music didn't come from the television but from a school band. The flowers weren't a funeral wreath but a memorial to fallen soldiers. It was Remembrance Sunday 1987.

No. Gareth must not wind up buried under piles of rubble as people had that day. No warning had been given then. This time one would be. She shouted at the empty store fronts as she raced past. "Bomb! There's a bomb!"

Then her feet faltered to a stop. Where was she? She didn't remember any of these shops. There should have been a cinema and a news agent. Then turn right and there would be the town square with the war memorial. The hotel was only a little farther on. It had to be.

Her sides heaved, and her lungs were bursting. But she could keep running. She could do anything to save Gareth. Her whole life— everything she cared about was in that hotel room that might explode into a million fragments at any moment. She must get to him. But which direction should she run?

She looked wildly up and down the deserted street.

Should she go back to the chip shop? By now she wasn't certain where it was. She thought she had only taken one turning. But she must have become confused and taken more.

She heard a car engine. Headlights approached from around a corner. She dashed into the street, waving her arms wildly. "Help! Please! There's a bomb—" The car roared by. They must not have even seen her.

At the foot of the street the car turned left. Did that mean there were people that direction? She had no better idea. She ran, her ears straining for the one sound she dreaded most—the tearing explosion that would tell her she was too late.

She headed up a new street, telling herself she had seen these buildings before. Sure she had. The tea shop was just in the next block. Maybe. She could find her way easily to the hotel from there. *Please, Lord. Please. Let this be right.*

But how long did she have? Worry circled in her mind. Maybe they would set the bomb to explode in the middle of the night. Of course, they would. In hopes of getting everyone while they slept. Or maybe they didn't want to kill people—just frighten them. Demonstrate the power of terror. Maybe the IRA would issue their own warning. Sometimes they did. Maybe a warning had already been sent. Gareth and all the guests could be safely away when she got there. She didn't even need to be doing this.

But no argument could stop her running. She sped around a corner, and there it was. How on earth did she get here? This was the back of the hotel. But, thank God, however she got here, it was still standing, tall and square against the black sky. She glanced upward at the top floor where Gareth's room was. There was a light in his window. "Gareth!" she shouted.

The alley door was unlocked. She stumbled into the black kitchen, sending pans crashing. She pushed through a swinging door and across the dining room. "Gareth!" She hit a table set for breakfast. Glassware shattered. The hotel was still. Her own voice echoed back at her as she sped up the narrow back stairway, screaming, sobbing, choking. "Gareth! Gareth!"

He would hear her. He would come. They would run. Together. Hand in hand. Away from this place of fear and violence. This would show Gareth she was right. He would come with her. They would be together just as she had dreamed. "Gareth! Gareth!"

Up another flight of stairs. How many more could there be?

"Mary!" Gareth's voice.

There he was—at the top of the next turning. They leaped toward each other. The next moment they were in each other's arms.

"A bomb! There's a bomb!" Even as she said it, she was starting back down, pulling at him. She wanted to explain, but there wasn't time. And she had no breath. Second floor. Around and down. First floor. Around and down. Back through the dining room.

Halfway across the kitchen, she stumbled into the pans she had scattered earlier. She grabbed wildly at the counter but couldn't stop her plunge. Gareth's arms came around her. He bent over to lift her to her feet.

The blast knocked them to the floor, Gareth on top of her.

Silence. Why was it so quiet? Then there was a great crash as pots, kettles, and crockery fell around them. As if in slow motion, she heard each thing clatter, bounce, and settle.

The wall beside them wavered and creaked, then split with a great crashing and pelted down over them.

Read Epoch 10 of The Celtic Cross series for the stunning conclusion to Mary and Gareth's odyssey.

HISTORICAL NOTE

The valiant work of the Society of Friends, or Quackers, is a matter of history. Against all odds, with only 3,000 members of the society in Ireland and a population of around eight million starving people, Quakers like Emelia Foxe worked tirelessly to raise awareness around the world and to feed the hungry with their own hands. Many died from famine-related illnesses themselves.

The British government followed the Quaker example by supplying famine pots (sometimes called workhouse pots) as well. Even the Sultan of Turkey sent pots to Ireland. Today there is a memorial to the famine pot in County Donegal. Many such pots have been discovered at country houses, such as Lissadell House in County Sligo. They are now often used as planters for flowers.

In one of those instances of fact following fiction—which seem to happen so often—The hotel bombing scene was based on my own stay in a hotel near Enniskillen, where, indeed, a funeral was taking place—but, thankfully, no bomb.

It was some time later that I learned of the bomb planted by the Continuity IRA that blew up the Killyhevlin Hotel in Enniskillen during a Catholic wedding in July of 1996. Even though a warning had been given, 17 people were injured.

REFERENCES

Part II, Ireland: The Pursuit of Peace

An Address to the Church of England Evidencing Her Obligations Both of Interest and Conscience to Concur with His Gracious Majesty in the Repeal of the Penal Laws and Tests. Pamphlet. 11 September 1688. Original is in Linen Hall Library.

Ashley, Maurice. *The Greatness of Oliver Cromwell.* New York: Macmillan, 1958.

Bardon, Jonathan. *A History of Ulster.* Belfast: Blackstaff, 1992.

Bennett, H.S. *English Books and Readers 1603-1640.* Cambridge: Cambridge Univ. Press, 1970.

Bishop, Patrick, and Eamonn Maillie, *The Provisional IRA*. London: Corgi, 1987.

The Book of Common Prayer. Eyre and Spottiswoode, 1968.

Buchan, John. *Oliver Cromwell*. Boston: Houghton Mifflin, 1934. Pp. 471-90.

Carson, John T. *God's River in Spate, the Story of the Religious Awakening of Ulster in 1859*. Antrim: W & G Baird. Second edition. Baird, 1994 "What's the News?": 121; Prayer Card: frontispiece; Decision Card: 125; Johnston's sermon: 57; "Oh, That Will Be Joyful": 58. Published by the Presbyterian Historical Society with the authority of the Board of Communications, Presbyterian Church in Ireland, Church House, Belfast.

The Case of the Protestant Dissenters of Ireland with Respect to the Sacramental Test Humbly Represented to the Legislature. Pamphlet. 1723. Linen Hall Library.

Christian Prayer: The Liturgy of the Hours. New York: Catholic Book, 1976. Source for graveside service in Epoch 9.

Coonan, Thomas L. *The Irish Catholic Confederacy and the Puritan Revolution*. Dublin: Clonmore & Reynolds, 1954.

Curtin, Nancy J. *The United Irishmen, Popular Politics in Ulster and Dublin, 1791-1798*. Oxford: Clarendon, 1994.

Dangerous Consequences of Repealing the Sacramental Test. Pamphlet. London: Roberts. Linen Hall Library.

Dolan, Josephine. *History of Nursing.* Philadelphia: Saunders, 1968. 320-21.

Elliott, Marianne. *Wolf Tone, Prophet of Irish Independence.* New Haven: Yale Univ., 1989.

Empey, Arthur Guy. *Over the Top.* New York: Putnam's, 1917.

Foster, R. F., ed. *The Oxford History of Ireland.* Oxford: Oxford Univ., 1989.

Fox, Charlotte Milligan. *Annals of the Irish Harpers.* London: Smith, Elder, 1911. Lyrics of Irish harp songs are based on this careful study, which was dedicated to "The Right Hon. The Earl of Shaftesbury, K.C.V.O., K.P., President of The Irish Folk-Song Society."

Fraser, Antonia. *Cromwell, The Lord Protector.* New York: Knopf, 1973.

Gilby, Thomas, editor and translator. *Saint Thomas Aquinas.* Philosophical Texts. New York: Oxford Univ., 1960.

Haire, Robert. *The Story of the '59 Revival with Some Methodist Sidelights.* Belfast: Nelson & Knox, n.d.

Haller, William. *The Rise of Puritanism.* New York: Columbia Univ., 1938.

Haythornthwaite, Philip. *The English Civil War 1642-1651.* N.p.: Gladford, 1983.

Higgins, Paul Lambourne. *John Wesley: Spiritual Witness.* Minneapolis: Denison, 1903.

Hone, Joseph. *W. B. Yeats.* London: Macmillan, 1942.

Kohfeldt, Mary Lou. *Lady Gregory.* New York: Atheneum, 1985.

Knox, John. *The Book of Common Order.* Vols. 4, 6. *The Works of John Knox* collected and edited by David Laing. Edinburgh: The Bannatyne Club, 1966. (Formal prayers in Epoch 7 were adapted from this source.)

Letter from a Distinguished English Commoner to a Peer of Ireland on the Repeal of a Part of the Penal Laws Against the Irish Catholics. Pamphlet. London: Keating, 1785.

Leyburn, James G. *The Scotch-Irish, a Social History.* Chapel Hill, N. C.: Univ. of North Carolina, 1962.

Lloyd-Jones, D. M. *The Puritans: Their Origins and Successors.* Edinburgh: Banner of Truth Trust, 1987.

Macdonald, Lyn. *Somme.* London: Joseph, 1983.

Macrory, Patrick. *The Siege of Derry.* Oxford: Oxford Univ., 1988.

Magee, John. *The Heritage of the Harp.* Belfast: Linen Hall Library, 1992.

Maguire, W. A. *Belfast.* Staffordshire, U. K.: Keele Univ., 1993.

Maxwell, Constantia. *In Ireland Under the Georges.* Dundalk: Dundalgen, 1949.

Irish History from Contemporary Sources, 1509-1610. London:Allen & Unwin, 1923.

Country and Town in Ireland Under the Georges. Dundalk: Tempest, 1949.

McCavery, Trevor. *Newtown: A History of Newtownards.* Belfast: White Row, 1994.

McConnell, Charles. *Carrickfergus: A Stroll Through Time.* Carrickfergus: Carrickfergus Publications, 1994.

McNeill, Mary. *The Life and Times of Mary Ann McCracken, 1770-1866.* Dublin: Figgis, 1960. I have been as accurate as possible as to the spirit of Mary Ann's biography. She was an energetic correspondent, and, although most of the letters in this novel are fictionalized, her passionate statements on the rights of women are taken from the first letter she wrote to Henry Joy in Kilmainham Jail on March 16, 1797 (p.127). Evan's letter is based on one William McCracken wrote to his sisters (p. 120). Mary Ann's comments on the Union are from a letter to her cousin (p. 202).

Middlebrook, Martin. *First Day on the Somme.* New York: Norton, 1972.

Miller, Perry, and Thomas H. Johnson. *The Puritans.* Vol. 1. New York: Harper & Row, 1938.

Millin, S. Shannon. *Sidelights on Belfast History.* Belfast: Baird, 1932.

Mitchell, T. Crichton. *Meet Mr. Wesley.* Kansas City, Mo.: Beacon Hill, 1981.

Montgomery, William of Rosemount. *The Montgomery Manuscripts, 1696-1706.* Extracted in "Glimpses of Old Newtownards," no.1, Ards Historical Society. Pamphlet. N.d.

Notestein, Wallace. *The English People on the Eve of Colonization, 1603- 1630*. New York: Harper & Brothers, 1954.

Packer, J. I. *A Quest for Godliness, The Puritan Vision of the Christian Life*. Wheaton, 111.: Crossway, 1990.

Phelan, Brian. "The Treaty." London: Thames Television/Screen Guides, 1991. Pamphlet. N.d.

Powell, S. *The Advantages Proposed by Repealing the Sacramental Test*. London: N.p., 1733.

Reid, William. *Authentic Records of Revival Now in Progress in the United Kingdom*. London: Nisbet, 1860. Reprint 1980, Wheaton, IL: Richard Owen Roberts.

Ryken, Leland. *Worldly Saints, The Puritans As They Really Were*. Grand Rapids: Zondervan, 1986.

Sheehan, Sean. *Dictionary of Irish Quotations*. Cork: Mercier, 1993.

Stevenson, John. *Two Centuries of Life in Down, 1600-1800*. Belfast: White Row, 1920.

Van Der Zee, Henri and Barbara. *William and Mary*. New York: Knopf, 1973.

Wesley, John. *Journal* and "The Case of Reason Impartially Considered." Sermon LXX from *The Works of John Wesley* on Compact Disc. Franklin, Tenn.: Providence House, 1995. I have put no words in John Wesley's mouth that were not his own.

Williams, J. B. "The Nineteenth Century and After." Periodical. Vol. 72, July-Dee 1912. London: Sampson Low.

Wilson, Gordon, with Alf McCreary. *Marie, A Story from Enniskillen.* London: Marshal Pickering, 1990.

Wilson, Ron. *A Flower Grows in Ireland.* Elgin, 111.: Cook, 1976.

Yeats, William Butler. *The Land of Heart's Desire.* New York: Macmillan, 1907.

"The Stolen Child," "The Lake Isle of Innisfree," "In Memory of Eva Gore-Booth and Con Markievicz," in *The Poems.* Edited by Richard J. Finneran. New York: Macmillan, 1983.

BOOKS BY DONNA FLETCHER CROW

Glastonbury, The Novel of Christian England
An Arthurian Grail search from the birth of Christ through the Reformation

The Celtic Cross Series
Part I, Scotland: The Struggle for a Nation

The Keeper of the Stone,
Of Saints and Chieftains: Saint Columba brings Christianity to Scotland
The Forger of a Nation,
Of Kings and Kingdoms: Kenneth MacAlpin unites the Picts and the Scots
The Refiner of the Realm,
Of Queens and Clerics: Queen Margaret reforms the court
The Vanquishers of Tyranny,
Of Priests and Patriots: William Wallace and Robert the Bruce triumph over tyranny

Part II: Ireland: The Pursuit of Peace

The Planting of Ulster,
Of visionaries and Builders: The Scottish settle the Plantations
The Hammering of the Inhabitancy,
Of Brothers and Strangers: Cromwell conquers Ireland
The Strife of Ascendancy,
Of People and Rulers: The English establish rule over the land and the church
The Shaping of the Union,
Of Plots and Parliaments: Ireland is united with England and Scotland
The Famishment of the People,
Of Hunger and Fulfillment: The story of the potato famine
The Dawning of Peace,
Of Dreamers and Designers: The Birth of Northern Ireland

(continued on next page)

The Monastery Murders, Clerical Mysteries

A Very Private Grave
Legendary buried treasure, a brutal murder and lurking danger—
an itinerary of terror across a holy terrain
A Darkly Hidden Truth
Ancient puzzles, modern murder and breathless chase scenes
through a remote, waterlogged landscape
An Unholy Communion
An idyllic pilgrimage through Wales becomes a deadly struggle between good and evil
A Newly Crimsoned Reliquary
Murder stalks the shadows of Oxford's hallowed shrines
An All-Consuming Fire
A Christmas wedding in a monastery—
if the bride can defeat the murderer prowling the Yorkshire moors
Against All Fierce Hostility
Is Felicity and Antony's spectacular train journey across Canada
carrying them away from murder—or toward it?

The Elizabeth & Richard Literary Suspense Mysteries

The Torch Ignites
Elizabeth and Richard's strife-filled first meeting in a New England autumn
The Shadow of Reality
Elizabeth and Richard at a Dorothy L Sayers mystery week high in the Rocky Mountains
A Midsummer Eve's Nightmare
Elizabeth and Richard honeymoon at a Shakespeare Festival in Ashland, Oregon
A Jane Austen Encounter
A second honeymoon visit to Jane Austen's homes turns deadly
A Most Singular Venture
Murder in Jane Austen's London

The Daughters of Courage Family Saga

Kathryn, Days of Struggle and Triumph
The unique story of Idaho's desert pioneers in the early days of the twentieth century.
Elizabeth, Days of Loss and Hope
Kathryn's daughter finds her way through the challenges of the Great Depression and World War II
Stephanie, Days of Turmoil and Victory
Strong family ties help Stephanie achieve success in the turbulent days of the 1970s

(continued on next page)

Lord Danvers Investigates, Victorian True-Crime Mysteries

A Most Inconvenient Death
The brutal Stanfield Hall murders shatter a quiet Norwich community
and pull Danvers from deep personal grief into a dangerous investigation.
Grave Matters
Lord and Lady Danvers' honeymoon in Scotland is interrupted
by the ghosts of Burke and Hare-style grave robbers.
To Dust You Shall Return
Catherine Bacon is murdered in the very shadow of Canterbury Cathedral
but Charles and Antonia are overwhelmed with their own problems.
A Tincture of Murder
William Dove is on trial in York for poisoning his wife while Lord and Lady Danvers struggle
to assist in a refuge home where fallen women continue to die mysteriously.
A Lethal Spectre
A glittering London season set against the horrors of an Indian mutiny

Where There is Love Historical Romance

Where Love Begins
Can Catherine Peronnet find God's purpose for her life
when her beloved Charles Wesley marries another?
Where Love Illumines
Mary Tudway must choose: a life of pleasure amidst London's high society
or a life of faith and service with the devout Rowland Hill?
Where Love Triumphs
Charming, brilliant and lame, Sir Brandley Hilliard believes he can do very well without
love of any kind in his life—until he meets Elinor Silbert—and then Charles Simeon.
Where Love Restores
Granville Ryder must struggle to find his place in his illustrious family, in God's work
and in Georgiana Somerset's heart
Where Love Shines
Blinded in the Charge of the Light Brigade, Richard, inspired by the Earl of Shaftesbury,
gropes through physical and spiritual blindness to the light of Jennifer's love
Where Love Calls
Kynaston Studd is on fire to carry the love of God to the ends of the earth with Hudson Taylor;
Hilda Beauchamp adds fuel to another kind of fire.

A Lighted Lamp,
Scenes of Christmas Through Time
A collection of short stories for holiday reading

ABOUT THE AUTHOR

Donna Fletcher Crow has written more than 50 novels drawing on her love for and study of the history and literature of the British Isles. Both of her previous epics, *Glastonbury*, the Novel of Christian England, and *The Fields of Bannockburn* (from which The Celtic Cross Series, Part I, was taken) were given top historical fiction awards by the National Federation of Press Women.

In writing *The Banks of the Boyne* (which furnished the basis for the Celtic Cross Series, Part II) she turned to the heritage of her husband's Irish family whose sixth great-grandfather was converted under the preaching of John Wesley in Ireland in 1787—a legacy that still burns bright more than 200 years later.

Donna also authors three mystery series: The Monastery Murders, clerical mysteries; Lord Danvers Investigates, Victorian true-crime Mysteries; and The Elizabeth and Richard literary suspense series. Donna and her husband of 57 years live in Boise, Idaho. They have 4 adult children and 15 grandchildren. She is an enthusiastic gardener.

To read more about all of Donna's books and see pictures from her garden and research trips, as well as subscribe to her newsletter, go to: www.DonnaFletcherCrow.com

You can follow her on Facebook at: Donna Fletcher Crow, Novelist of British History.

www.ingramcontent.com/pod-product-compliance
Lightning Source LLC
Chambersburg PA
CBHW020906160726
47993CB00005B/1835